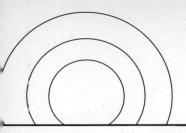

Cousins

APPLE SIGNATURE

VIRGINIA HAMILTON

Cousins

AN
APPLE
PAPERBACK

SCHOLASTIC INC.
New York Toronto London Auckland Sydney

No part of this publication may be reproduced in whole or in part, or stored in a retrieval system, or transmitted in any form or by any means, electronic, mechanical, photocopying, recording, or otherwise, without written permission of the publisher. For information regarding permission, write to Philomel Books, a division of The Putnam & Grosset Book Group, 200 Madison Avenue, New York, NY 10016.

ISBN 0-590-45436-6

15 14   1/0 2 3/0

Printed in the U.S.A.   40

Author photo by Jimmy Byrge

To Etta Belle Hamilton, 1892-1990

The Care

1 🌿 "You hear that?" Cammy asked Gram
Tut. "Otha Vance is building a hog house. And asking you to help him."

She thought she heard Gram Tut crow thinly. But
she wasn't sure. Gram was over there, in the bed by
the window. And the sound was like a rooster from
way across the barnyard.

Tut didn't turn her head to greet her grandchild.
She didn't move at all.

Cammy walked across the darkened room and
turned on the light above the sink. She tiptoed to
the bed, hopped up on the side rail and leaned
close. Gram Tut's eyes were closed. Already the
smell of the place, of old people, was up her nose.
Cammy smacked a big kiss on her grandmother's
cheek.

"There! I planted it, Gram. Now don't wash it.

Let it grow." Something about her Gram brought out the best in Cammy.

Tut couldn't wash her own face. "Poor old thing," Cammy's mama said.

You're not poor anything, Cammy thought, looking down at her Gram. She touched the lines of crisscross wrinkles on Gram's cheek. "You're my Gram and you need me to snuggle your face once in a while," she said.

Cammy didn't snuggle against Gram now. She would do that before she left. It always made Gram cry. But Gram Tut liked her to do that all the same.

"Gram?" Cammy leaned closer. Gram Tut's eyes were still closed. "You're not dead yet, are you?"

There was a long moment in which Cammy held her breath. But then, Tut gave a grin; said weakly, "Fooled ya!" and shot her eyes wide open.

It was a rough game that Tut managed to play with Cammy. Pretend dead-as-a-doornail was what Cammy called it. Gram Tut thought that was a riot. She was usually half awake when Cammy came. She would hear her granddaughter tiptoeing in and she would at once play dead.

"Don't tell Maylene," Tut had said. Maylene was Gram Tut's daughter and Cammy's mama. "She doesn't have a fingernail bit of humor in her."

They never played the game when anybody else was around.

Now, Cammy grinned. "Gram," she said, "you didn't fool me. I knew you was here, and always will be, too."

"Expect so, the rate I've been here," murmured Tut.

"Ninety-four years!" squealed Cammy.

"Oh, surely, not that long!" Tut said, softly.

Cammy let it go. "Gram Tut?"

What, honey? Tut's throat moved but she hadn't the strength right then to speak.

"Did you hear what I said? Otha Vance is building hisself a hog house . . ."

Him. Himself, honey. Not hisself, Tut thought. Doesn't Maylene or that school teach you a thing?

"He needs some help, Mister Vance says," Cammy explained. "Me and you could help him, if you want."

Cammy knew better than that. Mr. Vance lived at the Care, also. She knew he wouldn't build a hog house, nor could Gram Tut help him at anything. But it was part of the game, like saying to Gram, "What did you do today?" And Gram Tut saying back, "I'm worn out. I cleaned the whole house," when everybody knew she was mostly bedridden. She had no house now.

"Did you hear what I said, Gram?"

This time, Tut did get the words out before the strength left her completely. She hoarded her energy every morning after breakfast, knowing that Cammy would come see her later. And the child, talking a blue streak.

Tut's dry lips parted, "Tell that old fool he'll never make another pig sty . . . nor wallow in the mud-manure, either," Tut said. Her voice was just above a whisper, getting stronger, now that she had someone to talk to.

"I hate hogs," Cammy told her.

"But you love the sound of spareribs knocking . . . their taste in your mouth," Tut murmured.

"And with sourdough bread, good and hot, with the butter dripping out of it! Ooooh!" moaned Cammy.

"Mom has made her last meal on this earth," Cammy's mama, Maylene, had said one day about Gram Tut.

They all missed Gram Tut's cooking. When it first happened that she no longer could cook, before the Care, she would sit in the kitchen. Maylene would do the cooking with Tut at her elbow. "Put a little ketsup in with the chicken and flour. You don't need to fry it, Maylene. Do as I say," Tut would tell her. "Just stick it in the oven with a little vinegar and honey. You never do listen to what I tell you."

Her mama had to do it her way. Said the idea of ketsup and vinegar made her want to upchuck. She fried everything. The chicken she made, though, was all right. But greasy.

Not as good as my Gram doing it, herself, in the oven, Cammy thought now. Not never that good, yummy-yum.

"I always stir a little love and kisses into my food," Gram said.

Oh, Gram! "Maybe you can make us something

good-tasting for Christmas," sighed Cammy. And then: "You asleep?" Tut went in and out of sleep easily. Her mouth lay slack, drawn to one side of her face.

"That's no kind a Christmas dinner—chicken," Tut said, suddenly wide awake. She had been thinking about her summer curtains. Better had get them up, and the screens in, too. Get up just after dawn, before I start in baking pies. What month is it? Where am I? she thought. Oh.

It surprised Cammy when Gram's voice became so young and fresh.

"You want turkey and duck . . . for Christmas, like in the old times," Tut said. She remembered her Grandfather Sam shooting fox. Pretty little things.

"Truly, Gram? Will you come home when its Christmas and make it for us?" Cammy asked, all eagerness, forgetting that Gram was old and might not live that long.

"Child . . . you wear me out . . . in five minutes. I swept the grass . . . no . . . I swept the porch. I mean . . . the whole house. What more . . . where is Thy light!" Gram's voice quavered on the last words.

"Gram," Cammy said. She knew her Gram was helped out of bed twice a day for lunch and for dinner. She watched Gram Tut closely.

Sometimes, Gram's mind took a wrong turn, Maylene said.

Tut closed her eyes and opened them. Her gaze

wandered, found the portrait of her husband, Emmet, high up on the wall.

Gramper Em-un-Ems, Cammy had called him when she was five or six. Tut had thought that was so cute.

Now Tut was whispering at the portrait. Cammy thought she was speaking to her. "Don't talk, Gram, 'cause it wears you out. Just listen. I was telling you that Mister Vance wants your help. Hear him outside?" Cammy went on. "His chair squeaking? I think he's coming in now. Gram! Shall I let him come in?"

"Does he have his . . . pajama bottoms still on?" Tut said. Her voice had wheezed from her chest. She turned her eyes toward Cammy. She could turn her head sometimes. But she didn't then.

"Sure he has them on. They don't let him walk around silly," Cammy said.

"They say he takes his night clothes off all in the hallway," said Tut.

Cammy knew that had happened a month ago and hadn't happened since or she would've heard. Gram lost plenty of time. She could speed it up, though, when she felt like it.

"Let him on in," Tut said. "Mebbe he knows me today."

Cammy went to the door and directed Otha Vance in. She spoke grandly but in a soft voice so as not to alert the nurses. "My Gram will see you now, kind sir."

Otha Vance looked Cammy up and down, but didn't answer a word. He rolled in. He was a sagging, pale little man in a wide-brimmed farmer's straw hat, surrounded by his wheelchair. He had moist, beady eyes and no hair to speak of under the hat. He was kept in the chair by a sash around his waist attached to a harness across his shoulders. The harness and sash were tied together at the back of the chair.

Otha seemed to shrink farther into the chair each time Cammy saw him. He had stopped beside Gram's sink to take in her "home." He looked over at the television at the foot of the bed. It was tuned to a talk show. He gazed at the bed crank to judge Gram's condition today. The top of the bed was raised, an aid to keeping her lungs free of fluid.

"Got a cold?" he hollered. He never could speak softly. He didn't get an answer, either. He didn't expect any, and didn't listen, anyhow. He took in the bed last, with Cammy standing there on the railing. Her neck was craned around to watch him. She eyed him suspiciously.

Swiftly, Otha rolled up behind her and pinched her waist.

"Ouch! You old—I knew you were going to do that!" He had been so fast. Cammy made a spitball. Otha saw her mouth working and raised his hand to her. She parted her mouth just so he could see the spit a minute. He dropped his hand at that.

I'm eleven, Cammy thought. I know better than

to use a spitball on an old farmer in a wheelchair. But he don't know I know! Mom would whip my daylights out for doing something like that. Don't know what Andrew would do to me.

Andrew was Cammy's big brother. She was usually in his charge, when he could find her. He never told when she slipped off. It was his fault anyway, for not watching her closely enough. If he told their mama she'd run off, he'd have to admit he'd go looking for her only about half the time.

Andrew was sixteen and hard as nails, people thought. But Cammy knew better. Maylene had been warned by her own sister, Effie Lee, that Andrew could be a drinker. Cammy never ever told on him, either.

Otha gave Cammy one of his blind kind of looks, although he wasn't near blind. He wore glasses that were rimless and always so dirty, he might as well have been blind. He would fall down when he tried to stand on his feet. That was the reason he was tied in the chair. And he was too feeble to live alone any longer in his huge farmhouse. He'd fallen too often and couldn't get up by himself. His children moved him to the Care home.

"Got sixteen cent?" he was asking Tut.

"What for, Otha?" she said. "You forget how to say good morning to me?"

"Gram. It's after four o'clock in the afternoon, goodness sakes," Cammy told her.

"To get a bus so's I can go home," Otha said. "I'll give you a dollar if you call the law."

"What for?" asked Gram, breathless a moment.

"For to arrest that boy of mine. Putting me in here," Otha told her.

"There's no bus," Cammy cut in. "They don't run the bus hardly, least, not to your house. Anyways, your house is been sold."

"You better get outta here, little girl," he said. "Nurse! Nurse! The kid is messin' around!"

"Hush up, Otha," Gram said.

"Oh, be quiet! Don't see why everybody's so cranky," he said. "The wife's stayed away all day. Mad at me, too." He looked glum.

"He's forgot his Betty has passed," Maylene had told Cammy.

Her mama also said that it was weird the way Otha "fitted to his gravity," was the way she put it. Without warning, he would drop things and fall in a heap. Cammy had seen him standing in the door of his "home" once, that being what they called their rooms at the Care. Most residents had a "home" all to themselves. Some few men shared their "homes" in big, double rooms. But one time, somehow Otha blew himself forward like out of a cannon. He'd shot himself across the hall. His head hit the railing the elders held to when they walked, when they could walk, and which they pulled themselves along when they were in wheelchairs.

It hadn't hurt Otha. "Farmer," Maylene had said, "hard-headed as he can be."

Gram said, quietly, with her eyes closed, "So, Otha . . . what you . . . up to?"

"He's building a hog hut, I told you," Cammy said.

"Oh, will you be quiet?" Otha said. "I'm talking to your mother."

"No, you're not!" Cammy and Gram said almost at the same time.

Cammy squealed with laughter, just as Lilac Rose, the best attendant on the wing, stopped to study the three of them.

"Party time," she said, coming in to check on Gram Tut. "Hello there, Miz Tut," she said. "How's my favorite lady this afternoon?" She lifted the blanket and looked and felt under Tut to see if she was still "comfortable," was the way she put it. That meant dry, Cammy knew. Cammy turned her face away from what Lilac was doing. At the same time, she blocked Otha's view.

Gram Tut peered at Lilac Rose. They looked deeply of one another. Tut said not a word. Lilac Rose worked silently.

"Hi, Lilac, I love you," Cammy said, sweetly.

Lilac smiled. "Hi, baby. I love you, too," she answered.

"Don't tell on me, please?" Cammy pleaded.

"Huh. Haven't seen nobody," Lilac said, breezily. "Haven't heard nothing."

Anybody. Goodness. Haven't heard anything. Lordy, Tut thought.

"Thank you, Lilac," Cammy whispered. She placed her cheek on the brown coolness of Lilac's arm as Lilac took care of Gram. Lilac Rose never minded her and never told on her to a soul.

"I'm goin' tell," Otha said, peering around Cammy's back. "Kid!"

"Oh, Otha, get out of here! Don't always be so rotten," Lilac said. "Miz Tut likes having her grandbaby come visit."

"Well, I will, too, tell," Otha said. "There's nobody come to see me!"

"So whose fault is that?" asked Lilac Rose.

Otha wouldn't say. Perhaps he hadn't heard. For he backed his chair carefully to the door. All at once, he shot through the opening and across the hall. He held his feet high off the floor as the wheels spun in reverse. He hit the railing with full force. And gave out a hog call that Cammy could admire. It wasn't ear-splitting, though, like the kind the young hog callers could do at the county fair.

There was a thud as, quite by accident, the chair with Otha fell over on its side from the impact. The noise in the cool, dim hallway caused a stir, and cries of, "Help! Nurse! Somebody help me!"—up and down the wing.

"Oh, oh," Lilac said, under her breath. She went on about her business with Gram. She changed Tut's bed gown and turned her on her side facing the door. Then she gave a glance toward the hallway. "Better beat it, Cammy," she said. "In a few minutes, I've got to get your Gram up for supper, too."

Miss Mimi across the hall came wheeling out of her home. She peeked out to see if Otha was all right. Her hair was rolled in a fresh pompadour. Lipstick and rouge prettied her face. She gave Otha the once-over, as if he were some alien, iron bug wiggling on its side. Then, she wheeled on by him down the hall. "I'm coming girls, don't fret," she called.

Tut sighed, said to the air, "We take care of . . . our own, don't we?"

The nurse's station wasn't far up at the center of long corridors to the three wings. In a minute, ladies in white would be all over the place, Cammy thought. She said so to Lilac. "But shouldn't you go pick Mister Vance up?"

Go pick *up* Mister Vance, honey. Maylene hasn't taught you a thing, Tut was thinking.

"Honey, it'll take two at least to get him and that chair up off the floor," Lilac said, dryly. "If I try to move him, they'll say I oughtn't've. Shoulda waited for a nurse. Next thing, they'll turn around and yell at me for not helping him."

Still, Cammy thought Lilac should have gone to help him. She couldn't be seen out there to go, herself. He could have been hurt bad.

Lilac had started combing Gram's hair as best she could. Cammy watched. "One day, I comb it while she's lying like this," said Lilac. "Next time, I comb it after she's in the chair."

Now they heard feet scurrying.

"That way, in a couple of times, I get most of it done," Lilac went on.

Otha began shouting, "Somebody! Somebody!"

"All right, Otha, we're coming," somebody called.

"Better had fade away, honey," said Lilac.

"Can't I stay? I could hide under the bed," Cammy whispered, her eyes darting. "I could say my mama just went to the restroom, if anybody sees me.

"It could be a pool nurse," Cammy added. The pool nurses came in a rotation from the nearby hospitals. "They wouldn't know who I was."

"It's not the weekend," Lilac said. "Best you scoot."

Cammy waited by the sink. Ida, the nurse, and Dave, the assistant, were bent over Otha, examining him and asking him questions. Soon they had him upright in his chair and in his room. Otha shouted one second and moaned the next, as they closed the door.

Cammy went back to Gram, climbed up on the railing and said a hurried good-bye. "See you tomorrow," she said. She snuggled Gram's face.

Don't go! Tut thought. Need you to climb back up with my curtains.

"Gram? I love you best!" Cammy whispered into Gram's ear. More than Mama? she thought. Well, just as much.

"Don't go!" Gram Tut wailed.

"Now, now," Lilac soothed. "Shhh. Shhh, darlin'."

"Don't go." The whole night is coming. Tut could feel it creeping up on her. Big tears slid down her face.

"Oh, now, Miz Tut, everything's going to be fine," said Lilac. "I'm here and you'll soon be up in your chair, ready for your good supper."

Cammy was out of the room. She shut down her insides against Gram Tut's crying. And slipped away toward the big glass door at the end of the hall.

Glad it's Lilac with Gram, she thought. Shameful that my sorry cousins don't come to visit her some. Patty Ann. Richie. Glad the Care's not a bad place, though, like some they say are.

Cammy sighed. Don't see how anyone can taste food that's all ground into soupy-runny, she thought. Gram's got her false teeth. They just don't want to take time for her chewing slow. Some dumb supper.

2 🌿 Beyond the glass door was bright sunshine and summer. Shade trees and woods surrounded the Care on three sides. Outside, Cammy wondered why all of the folks didn't just walk on away and live under the trees in the woods. Now and then, one of them would go off looking for the house they once owned. But after a couple of times, they didn't wander anymore. She knew why.

"They just get lost. They don't have a place to go," she whispered. Some of them like Gram Tut can't get up and out under their own power, she decided. I know something. I bet if I could drive a bus, I could take a lot of 'em on out of there.

Where would I take them, where would they all go? She couldn't think of a place to take them. But then, she did.

"I'll lead them off into the thickest trees. I'll be the Pied Piper! Or Moses!" Cammy grinned.

She thought of a big tent amongst tall maples where they could all stay and have birthday parties. With that many old folks, there'd probably be a birthday party every day. She loved parties. But any party she'd ever had, had been just awful. She was working on having a good one, though. Maybe someday, she thought.

Cammy took a deep breath. No sunlight now. Hot today, maybe over ninety, she thought. You couldn't tell in the Care, in the rooms, which were air conditioned. There was a long rumble of thunder not far off.

Ooh! I hate thunder! She began to run. She had to cross the grassy space inside the oval drive of the Care. Then she hit the street in front of the Health Center. On down the road there and across the avenue. She looked both ways. It was then she sensed the dark clouds and forced herself not to look at them. There was no way she could not see the gray light. Before she knew it, there were a few drops of rain.

Darn!

She watched, half scared, as low, slithery rain clouds sped overhead faster than the fluffy white clouds they blotted out above them.

Fascinating, she thought, getting up her courage, and stuck her nose in the air.

The clouds whipped from the west, the direction she was going.

Then, she felt the wind on her face. And the rain came down with a wallop, falling into her eyes.

Ooh! Mama? Oh, it's going to get lightning on me!

The lightning lit the way. Thunder made her knees buckle. She was scared and felt alone in the world.

Cammy knew better than to take shelter under one of the shade trees along the road. But it looked dry under there.

It looks so safe! she thought.

She was feeling a little sick to her stomach. She would have cried in the next minute, ready to race for a large pine tree along the road. But then she realized where she was.

Oh, my goodness! Well, thank my lucky stars.

The drenching rain was running down her socks and into her sneakers. She was soaked. In one leap up a set of wood steps, she was on a familiar porch of a house painted sky blue with white trim. She stood there, hunched against the screen when a hand unlocked it and hauled her inside.

"Thanks, Aunt Effie," Cammy said.

"Anybody out in a storm like this on foot hasn't got good sense," Aunt Effie said, by way of greeting. She didn't smile.

Cammy would have explained that she'd been inside at the Care when she caught herself in time. Aunt Effie never gave her the chance, anyway.

"Don't stand there dripping on my rug. Here." Effie, her mama's oldest sister, flung a bath mat at her.

Cammy felt so ashamed. Orphan. She dropped

the mat and quickly stepped on it, wishing she could just disappear. If she just could, she would escape out the door. Eyes downcast, she caught a glimpse of the massive couch and twin club chairs under sleek plastic covers. Cost a fortune, her mama said.

"Give me your wet clothes," Effie demanded. She shut the front door. She made Cammy undress right there on the mat clear down to her undershirt and pink panties, and took her socks and sneakers.

"I'm putting this whole mess in the dryer," Effie said, "even though they're none too clean. See that you tell my sister that your Aunt Effie took care of her child. I'd never work so much that I'd have to leave my own child with just a sixteen-year-old *boy*!"

Meaning my brother, Andrew, Cammy thought. Bet you hate him even more than you hate me. Aunt Effie wouldn't know how to do a day's work, Mama says.

Chin on her chest, Cammy felt close to tears again. Why couldn't everybody be nice? She sighed in a deep breath.

Her undershirt was white with a tiny hole in front. Didn't match her panties at all. Cammy folded her arms over herself and tried not to shiver. She wasn't cold. Just clammy.

She heard her sneakers clomping in the dryer, from the kitchen. Hope they don't tear up my blouse, she thought.

"Don't sit down in just your underwears." Effie was back, acting like a dump truck, Cammy thought.

"I wasn't going to . . ."

Effie pushed a towel at her. "You can dry off with that and sit on it, too. You may sit in there but don't bother her."

The door was closed to "in there." Cammy had to leave this front room and go through a short, dark hall to another door, then open it to get to the sacred "in there."

Funny, she hadn't noticed the sound until Aunt Effie said that she wasn't to bother *her*. Now Cammy heard it.

Wouldn't it be nice if her cousin would vaporize the way people did on *Star Trek*? Beam me up, Scotty! Cammy thought. Coo-el if little *her* beamed up to a big blue star or to the moon or somewhere.

"Well, go on," Effie said. And as Cammy got up and went, Effie added, "Your legs is ashy. Tell your mama to buy you some hand cream."

I've got some, you fat pig! I hate hogs! Cammy thought.

She went in there and the sound floated around the room. It bounced off the walls and, softly, down from the ceiling.

Cammy took a seat behind the piano player, who was her cousin, Patricia Ann. She held the towel tightly around her shoulders. It fitted over her head like a hood. Cammy sighed into the music, which was nice. But it made her feel just so tired. She looked at Patricia Ann's long, crinkly hair, so pretty, way down her back. It was the color of maple syrup left in the sun. It was let out from her usual long French braid. Patty Ann's hair always was out on the day of her piano lesson. She must've had her lesson and was now practicing.

Can you wonder? Cammy thought. A kid comes home from her lesson and *practices*? When she took lessons once, Cammy never thought of practicing until a day or two before the next lesson.

"Oh, Patty Ann does everything just right," Cammy's mama said. "Effie sees to that. I never saw a child more afraid of somebody than that baby is of my own sister. Cammy, you should feel sorry for your cousin."

"I hate her," Cammy had said.

"Well . . ." Maylene said no more. Cammy was used to her mama not finishing what she would start to say.

Patricia Ann didn't turn around from the piano until she finished another song after the one she'd been playing when Cammy came in. She had to have heard Cammy come in. But Patty Ann wouldn't be disturbed until she had practiced her entire lesson.

The whole time, Cammy sat there, clutching the towel around her and trying to get the ash off her legs by rubbing her feet down them. All she managed to do was spread dirt to her calves and ankles.

She kept it up anyway. She couldn't sit still. Being there with her cousin made her as angry as she could be.

Good at everything, Cammy thought to Patty Ann's back. In school, at home, at her piano. Miss Goody-goody. Well, I am also good in lots of things, Andrew says.

The music stopped abruptly. Patty Ann turned the page of a small notebook next to her music. The page was blank. She'd come to the end of her lessons. She closed the book. Closed her music books, too. She closed the piano top over the piano keys. To Cammy, everything she did was like chalk scraping on a blackboard. The way Patty Ann looked, even her expression, made Cammy fit to be tied.

Patty Ann slid around on the piano seat. Facing Cammy, she turned her head to one side. After the first glance, she wouldn't look directly at Cammy.

"What in the world happened to you?" Patty Ann asked. Her voice was surprising, a low, husky alto. Naturally, she was a good singer, too. Patty Ann touched her new plaid dress. It was shades of wine, yellow and soft green with blue. It had a pleated skirt.

To look at it made a lump grow in Cammy's throat. She decided just to shrug her shoulders. A few seconds later she couldn't keep her mouth shut. "I got wet," Cammy said.

"I figured that!" Patty Ann said. She touched the

gold locket around her throat and the gold bracelet on her right wrist. She had a watch with a black leather band on her left wrist. "I knew it was going to rain even before my lesson was over. I could smell the rain in the air. I always can," Patty Ann said.

She swung her legs from one side of the piano bench to the other. This way, Cammy was sure to catch her full effect. Patty Ann's face was made even prettier by the wine shade of her dress. Carefully, she crossed her ankles so as not to touch her wine-colored socks with her patent-leather shoes.

Lordy, Cammy thought. "Do you always have to get so dressed up for your lessons? I mean, can't you ever relax?" Cammy asked.

Patty Ann raised her eyebrows. "Ho-hum, I am relaxed," she said. "Some people I know wouldn't never know how to be relaxed in pretty clothes, if they ever had any pretty clothes."

Cammy's ears felt hot. Anger flashed in her eyes. "You know what you look like in that brand new dress?"

"It's not so new," Patty Ann said. "I've had it a week. Mama says not every girl can have a dress like this because it costs high. You know, *expensive*. She says but I'm not just every girl."

You're trying to make me feel small, Cammy thought. Well, you won't!

"You look like death," Cammy told her. "Like you are going to a funeral, which is your own."

Once she got started, she couldn't stop herself. She saw Patty Ann's mouth turn down. "You look like a skeleton. I've never seen anybody that bony outside of a Halloween white cardboard skeleton."

"You are so jealous just because I can sit on my hair and I get all A's," Patty Ann remarked. "I got my picture in the paper for never having below a B plus, and you have *never* had your picture in the paper." She said this while looking out of the window and swinging her legs. Her voice was up high on itself but still husky.

"They'll spread your hair out on that little satin pillow," Cammy went on, heart beating fast. "They'll pin your eyelids back with glue and make your eyeballs look down at some toy piano in your lap. They'll break your fingers to curl them so it looks like you are playing the keys."

Cammy even shocked herself with her own meanness.

"You are just so stupid," Patty Ann said. "It's your loved one, Gram Tut, that smelly old bag of bones, that's dying."

"You shut up!" Cammy whispered. They had both been talking softly, in case Aunt Effie passed by the door.

"If you weren't so dumb," said Patty Ann, "you'd know she's gone into a fate-all position."

"A fate—what?" Cammy said, alarmed. She didn't know what a fate-all position was. Never had heard of it. "You take that back!"

"It's true. She's beginning to curl up like an unborn baby," Patty Ann said. "That's the way real old folks do before they pass away.

"And by the way," added Patty Ann, staring down her nose at Cammy, "where are your clothes, did you forget to wear them? Or did they just rot off you?" Patty Ann turned on Cammy in triumph.

Cammy got to her feet. If she ever doubted that Patty Ann was some enemy cousin, she didn't now. She shook her head. "You are trying to make me mad and you use Gram Tut, which is no fair. She's old," Cammy said.

"By now, she's about dead, too," Patty Ann said.

"Stop it!"

"You stop it. You started it."

Cammy smiled, her heart swelling for Gram Tut. "I know all about you," Cammy said, quietly. "I know what you do in the bathroom when you think nobody can see."

Patty Ann grew still. Cammy knew she ought to stop, but she couldn't help it. She had to finish, for Gram Tut's sake. "You stick your finger down your throat," Cammy said. "You force up all the food old Aunt Effie makes you take for lunch to camp. Kids say you did that a couple times last week. I know all about you."

Patty Ann's chest heaved. She looked sickly thin and strange to Cammy. Tears filled her eyes.

Cammy went on, although her heart wasn't in it. What good was it if Patty Ann was going to cry?

"You think you are fat. You're afraid of your own mama, afraid of doing anything wrong. That's why you get all A's. Andrew said so. You're afraid of what mean Effie will do to you if you don't. Wonder what she'd do if she knew you upchucked your food on purpose."

Patty Ann covered her face with her hands and sobbed.

"I don't care," Cammy said. "You just better learn to keep your mouth off Gram Tut, you hear? You don't say nothing bad about her or I'll come while you're asleep and cut your hair off!"

Patty Ann screamed, "Mooooother!" at the top of her lungs. She ran for the door but Cammy beat her to it. Cammy heard Aunt Effie upstairs, heading for the steps.

Cammy forced Patty Ann away with a thrust of her hip. She got out of there and sprinted to the kitchen. She turned off the dryer and got her clothes out.

"What's going on?" cried Effie, coming down the stairs.

"She made fun of me, Mother," Patty Ann called.

"Heifer," she heard Aunt Effie say.

I'm outta here! Cammy flew out the back door, clutching her clothes in her arms. She forgot about the missing bottom cement step and fell to her knees. "Ouch!" She got right back up, though, no matter that the pain was awful.

She came around the house just as Aunt Effie

with Patty Ann on her heels burst from the screen door. But by then, Cammy was on the street and on her way. They couldn't catch her, she didn't think. Oh-my-lordy! Aunt Effie was coming across the lawn. Cammy sprinted away.

The still warm clothes in her arms made her all hot and sweaty. She ran around some trees and dressed behind a tree trunk. Lordy, what if folks have seen me out here half nekkid? she thought. They'll just think I have on a swimsuit.

Cammy looked around to see where Aunt Effie was. She held her breath to listen. But it seemed Effie hadn't gone any farther than the curb.

Cammy got everything back on again. Even her sneakers. It was then she noticed it was still raining and she was wet all over again. Well, let lightning hit me, I don't care, she thought. She was burning mad, boy. Anything's better than that enemy place! she thought.

She raced the weather halfway home. A truck was coming toward her and slid to a stop next to her, spraying puddle water practically over her head. She recognized the two guys inside and grinned. Stuck her thumb out, real sassy. The door opened on the passenger side and a strong arm hauled her in. Today, it seemed that people were hauling her, one way or another.

Long Sleek Roads

3 🌿 Andrew called the pickup his pup. It was named P'up for short by the car maker, he told Cammy. And it was smaller than a full-size pickup. It was spiffy and Andrew drove it fast down roads shining almost forever. Silver band roads. It could still be raining, or storming, too. Andrew didn't mind. He liked the way the tires sounded on the wet blacktop. He was a good driver, even though he was only sixteen. He never drove too fast in a storm; he didn't slow down, either.

"You watch. That child's in for some serious trouble," Aunt Effie said to Maylene. "No boy at that age has any business with a car."

Cammy had been right there. What she forgot about the conversation, Andrew remembered. "Shows how much she knows—it's not *even* a car," later Andrew told Cammy. "And I'm not any *boy*," he said. "I'm a young adult."

"My dad gave me the pickup as a gift," he told Aunt Effie, "so you just mind your business." She didn't scare him one bit.

But she went on just as if he weren't there. That was the insulting part, Cammy's mama said later. "Oh, I know all about his *dad*," Effie said. "His big-shot dad's too good for this town and this family."

"All right, Effie, that's enough," Maylene told her.

"You better keep your mouth off my father," Andrew told Aunt Effie, "or I'll tell you all about *your* own self, too."

Cammy recalled how shocked she had been at her brother's boldness.

"Disrespectful. Just smart aleck," Aunt Effie said.

"I've never known another family that is always at one another, like this one," Maylene said. "Effie, you started it and it's finished, now. Not another word."

But Effie went on. She said it was up to her to say something when her own son was sitting in a cheap truck, in the death seat next to a sixteen-year-old driver.

"Nobody's making Richie ride in my pup," Andrew told her.

"If you didn't have it, he couldn't ride in it!" Aunt Effie had shot back.

And then Cammy's mama said something about what were they supposed to do. "Not have any transportation? Not ride for fear something bad *might* happen?" Maylene had said.

In the pup now with her brother, Cammy couldn't help smiling. Old Maylene was something. Cammy felt bold, calling her own mama "Old Maylene"!

Cammy was fairly soaked again from the rain. Andrew had reached over and hauled her up off the road. She'd climbed over Richie to take a seat in the middle.

Andrew'd brought a towel for her, too. And turned on the heat a moment over their cousin Richie's protesting. "It's too hot for heat, man. It's summer—man?" Whining Richie, Aunt Effie's only son. He was in the passenger seat by the window.

"My sister's wet, dork," Andrew told him. "She'll catch a cold and I'll get blamed."

"I'd blame Richie before I'd blame you," Cammy said.

"Swell," said Richie.

Andrew laughed. Then he said, "You ran off, Cam. I don't fashion that."

"Were you driving around looking for me?" she asked.

"Sure," he said. "Had to find you before Mom got home."

"You're not mad at me?" she asked.

He smoothed her hair back with the towel, as he drove, drying it more. "Oh, you're about up to par today, kid," he said. "Who could get mad at that? And getting yourself wet in a storm."

"I got soaked before now," she told him, explaining about Aunt Effie.

"No kidding, she came after you?"

"Great," Richie said. "Now she'll get on me for being around you guys."

"Aunt Effie and that brat sister of yours are both *weird*, Richie," Cammy said.

"Maybe Aunt Effie will forget about telling Maylene," Andrew said, "but I doubt it." He thought it amusing to call his mother by her first name. Maylene didn't think it was.

The conversation hung on the air. Richie didn't like the way Aunt Effie was, either, so he said. They couldn't get along for more than five minutes. Still, he didn't care to hear his cousins talk about her.

Andrew and Cammy knew that. Her brother gave her a look and she knew to stop talking about Aunt Effie.

The sky was bright gray at the storm's edge. Just a line of blue showing, but more to come. Cammy had her head on Andrew's shoulder. Her legs were crossed like a grown-up girl. Her knees stung where she had fallen. She tried to forget about it, resting her hands easily in her lap. Richie had his window open and Cammy's shoulders were getting chilly.

"I want to go home," she said, looking up at Andrew. "I'm pretty wet and cold. I think I scraped my knees some."

Andrew glanced over at Richie. She heard Richie's window roll up.

She was turned to Andrew. "Andrew?" she said.

"Shhh," he said. He was listening to the radio.

Some song about "You drive me crazy when I'm with you." She didn't much care for love songs. Andrew seemed to like them; Richie, too. They would stop what they were saying to listen when a love song came on. Like they were trying to learn something.

"Dumb stuff," Cammy said, under her breath.

"So, Gram Tut was okay today?" Andrew asked her, when the song was over.

"I don't know," Cammy said. "I guess. She talked some. Old Man Vance came in and bothered us."

If Cammy had known her brother was going to ask, she would have been ready. She would have had time to close herself off from how she felt about Gram Tut. From how she loved her just to death and hated Patty Ann for teasing so mean.

Old, funny Gram, I love you much! She missed coming home to find her Gram in the rocking chair, snapping some beans.

"You are snappy, yourself, just like them green beans," she'd told Gram.

And Gram said, "Those green beans, child. Don't they ever teach you the proper English in school?"

Cammy's eyes filled with tears. She sniffled and moaned a high, sad sound.

"Come on now, Cam, don't do that," Andrew told her. He put his arm around her shoulder, patted her.

"Andrew, Gram Tut's going to die!"

"No she's not," he said. "Least, not for a long time."

"She's old!" Cammy cried.

"Well, there's lots of old people," he said. "They walk around every day and they're all not going to pass on tomorrow."

"No, but . . ."

"No buts, Cammy. I swear, Gram Tut's not about to go anyplace just yet," Andrew said.

"When's the last time you saw her?" Cammy asked.

He was quiet a moment. "Last Sunday," he lied. He couldn't bear to see his Gram wasting away like that. "On my way over to see Dad."

At the mention of their dad, Cammy sat up straighter and wiped her eyes on the back of her hand. She had the feeling he could see her. He listened to every word she said. Cammy never could say about her father. She'd been so young when he first was out of the house. When he came over now, a rare event, she just sort of circled around him, stared at him, said nothing much to him. Sandy hair and light eyes. Not that she felt there was something missing at home. But she suspected he fit somewhere between their days and nights. A shadow something, before dawn and after sundown.

"I haven't seen Gram Tut in six months," Richie said. "Mom don't ever say Patricia Ann has to go see her."

Cammy remembered something Patty Ann had said. "Andrew, is it true that Gram Tut is in a fate-all position?" She thought that was the way Patty Ann had said it.

"A what?" Andrew and Richie both asked.

"A fate- or fete-all position? It sounded like," Cammy said. "Patty Ann told about it."

"It's a place to die in, you mean?" Richie said.

But Andrew was grinning; then, he caught himself. "S'nothing for you to worry about," he told Cammy. "You just go visit Gram Tut anytime you want to. Anybody bother you, tell 'em to come see me. Tell Gram Tut I said hi and I miss her, too."

Richie made up reports about having seen Gram Tut to please Aunt Effie. Patty Ann knew he was lying. She told Cammy; then, she was sorry she had.

Everybody knew Richie was a barefaced liar. Andrew said that Richie would lie about anything even when there was no reason for him to lie. Like the time he said he helped rob the bank in downtown Dayton. He had a lot of money suddenly and spread it all around about being a robber. The police came and took him away. He was back the very next day, after Aunt Effie proved he had been with her brother working on constructing a playground—the only job he ever held for more than a week. Lasted a month before he didn't show up one day, and the next and the next.

Richie made up large stories, "exaggerations,"

Cammy's mama called them. Andrew said Richie didn't mean anything bad by doing it. He said Richie felt anxious all the time and couldn't help himself from making up things to make himself feel better.

Andrew drove steadily, barely moving the wheel. Long sleek roads. Cammy sat up straight so she could see out the window. Fog had risen off the highway now from the rain, and hung above it. It swirled in the fields on either side of them, like white steam, rolling. Sunlight broke through low clouds. What rain there was, was misty. Then, the sun grew hot through the windshield. Andrew and Richie rolled down their windows. The breeze was warm. Hot sunlight ate up the clouds right before their eyes.

"Let's go home, I'm hungry," Cammy said. "Mama will want to know where I am."

"She's not home, yet. We've got time," Andrew said, mildly. "Here, look in the glove compartment. Candy bar."

"Coo-el!" Cammy said, reaching in. It was a BabyRuth. She loved BabyRuths.

"Anyway, I have to drop Richie someplace," Andrew said.

"Someplace where?" she asked. "Ummm, good!" she said, chewing.

"Someplace where he can go see about a job," her brother said.

"But it's about time for stores to close," she said.

"Night shift," Richie said. "Anyhow. You got to wait on line."

"Huh?" She didn't understand. The radio was loud. They were listening to songs again. She realized she had been shouting when she talked. They all were. The car was full of music swinging out the windows.

Prob'ly scares the cows and horses in the fields, Cammy was thinking.

They took the country roads, way out; and then came back. Cammy sensed they'd made a big square, going out where there were many houses. Whole 'burbs. And on the way back, they came to a great, huge, automotive place.

"It's a car mall," she piped up.

"It's a truck plant," Andrew said.

"Wow!" Cammy said. There were hundreds of people. They made kind of a line but the people were sitting or lying down. They had blankets and small tents and thermoses.

"What is going on—a midnight picnic?" Cammy said.

"Cool it, will you?" Richie said. "This is how you get a job." He took up a paper bag he had between his legs and turned it up to his lips. Cammy saw the neck of a bottle.

Swell, she thought. Richie offered the bag to Andrew, looking past her as he did so. "Gimme some, then," she said, by way of a joke. They ignored her. It was then she saw Richie's eyes were red-rimmed and crusty. The whites of his eyes looked full of blood. His hands trembled and his breath could knock out a bunch of old folks.

Andrew wasn't having any of the bottle. Shook his head. Richie screwed the top back on and stuck the bag and all into his jacket pocket.

That surprised her. She turned to her brother, stared at him. She was deciding something. He wouldn't look at her.

"Thought it was you, Mama did, drinking," she said. "It's not, is it?"

"Just close your face," Andrew told her. Hard as nails. It hurt her when he spoke like that. She hadn't expected it. He was being so nice to her.

But she knew something. It was Richie had the alcohol, she was pretty sure, and not Andrew. Glad of that, she thought. He, Richie, who sometimes left his paper bag in the glove compartment and Andrew probably forgot to get rid of it. Her mama found the bags with their empty bottles and thought it was Andrew.

"That crowd's not going to get any smaller, Richie," Andrew said.

"Man, you want me to stay out here all night, and I haven't got even a rock for a pillow?"

"All night?" Cammy said.

"You got a blanket and they'll let you inside if it gets too damp or rainy out," Andrew said.

"You have to sleep on the ground?" she asked.

They weren't hearing her. They talked over her, as though she weren't there.

"Look how long the line is," Richie whined. "I'll never even make the door before the end of the day tomorrow!"

"This is the only way, Richie. You have to wait in line and fill out an application."

"Man, what's the use? They ain't going to call. I've stood in umpteen lines and they never even know who I am when I try to find out something."

"No, because you never get your name on the lists!" Andrew said. "I've got my name on four different plant lists."

"But you already work for Dell's Oil Change and Tune-up," she said.

Andrew sighed. "Come on, Richie," he said.

"Man!" Richie cried. But he got out of the truck.

"You stay here," Andrew told her, as she made to follow Richie. Richie slammed his door on her. So she leaned out the window, sitting on her feet so she could see better.

All so many people. Andrew got a blanket out from the truck locker. He threw it over Richie's shoulder. Richie staggered. Cammy thought he must be kidding. Then, he side-stepped and fell on one knee.

"Man, Richie, straighten up!" Andrew whispered loud.

Richie laughed. He reached for his jacket pocket and what was there.

"No, you don't," Andrew told him. He yanked out the paper bag with its contents and took it to the truck.

Richie stretched out on the ground. He had a silly grin as he spread the blanket over him and folded it over his arms.

"Come on, Richie, get over in line," Andrew said. He sounded tired to Cammy.

"I'm making my own line," Richie said. "Gimme my taste back, Andrew."

"You're not getting any more, Rich. Don't act stupid. You'll catch somebody's attention in a minute. You have to wait in line!" Andrew said.

"I'm waiting, man," Richie said. "It don't matter where I wait." He laughed.

Andrew looked away to the crowd and then back to Richie again. His face kind of broke into pieces like he might cry.

Cammy couldn't believe he was going to cry. My brother? He stood there, looking at the ground. He shook his head and took deep breaths, sighs. She wondered if he and Richie would get into a fight. She wouldn't mind seeing her brother wipe out dumb Richie once.

Grab Richie up with one hand, Cammy thought. He needs a good shaking. Swing him around Andrew's head and let him loose. That would be something!

She smiled; looked aside before she got to giggling. So many people made her think they were all looking at Andrew and Richie, and then at her there in the pup.

Suddenly, Andrew started to walk away. Then,

he seemed to change his mind, and he came back. "I'm going but I'll be back later on, in a few hours, Rich. Okay?" she heard him say.

Richie had his eyes closed. Cammy could see he wasn't too happy. He barely nodded.

She watched as her brother came back to the truck. He had his head down and his hands in his pockets. She opened the door for him before he could do it.

"Thanks," he said, getting in.

"You're welcome," she said, proud she had a brother like him. "But why so many people?" she asked, once he was settled. "Why don't they all have jobs and stuff?"

"Some do," he said. "Some are looking for full time. Some just need work. Lot of people need jobs. This ain't the best of times."

"No?" she said. Well, she knew it wasn't. But most of the time everything looked pretty good to her. "You kidding me?" she asked.

"No," he said. "Lots of people don't have dads like we have that can help them out with work. We're lucky. I'm lucky. We're all lucky that Dad's nice enough to help Mom out still."

We're lucky, she repeated in her head, in Andrew's voice. But she didn't quite see what lucky was, when you weren't Patty Ann with new clothes all the time.

Andrew started the truck. It sputtered a moment before it sounded smooth, like it was ready to roar down the street. When they did start, Andrew eased the car along. They went slowly home down country roads. Cammy rolled down her window and stuck her head out a minute. She put her hand out in the air, let the air fill her palm and knock it back.

"Careful," Andrew told her. "Branches stick way out over the road, sometimes."

"Oh," she said. She sat up straight, both hands in her lap.

4 They went home. Andrew took his time and Cammy loved that, to get to ride with him by herself. Everything was okay between them. They were on each other's side.

They lived on the west side of town. Andrew swung the truck the long way around. The country road they came in on passed right by the cemetery, which was Dale Forest Cemetery. It didn't have a forest to it anymore. Cammy's mama said that long ago, trees had been cut down two by two to make way for graves. Gramper Em-un-Ems stayed in Dale Forest. It all made Cammy shiver, to think about him in his *grave*. She fought against the next thought, but it came through on its own and she couldn't stop it. Gram Tut would stay right next to Gramper one day. Her bed was already made and paid for, her mama told her. Awful.

They went by the pond. There were a great lot of ducks swimming and waddling, sitting in the shade right by the pond. It belonged to well-off folks who let you climb on the fence and feed the ducks. The ducks were beautiful. Andrew went slowly so she could see them. There was a low waterfall. In winter, the pond would freeze over and all the kids would ice skate. Except for her, and some few others around town, she guessed. Her mama was afraid of the pond and for the children maybe skating on thin ice.

Andrew took the truck to the right and onto Highway 68. They went through the main street of town, which was Ames Avenue. There was one main business street and this was it.

There were three stop lights on the Avenue. The first had a Dairy Queen with outdoor benches and tables, right there on the main drag where anybody coming into town could see you sitting. It was nice, sitting there; it was like saying, this is my town. She did that, sometimes. Had a sundae and sat right there practically under the stoplight. There was the Post Office and Laughing Pizza across the street from the Dairy Queen. A Sohio station and a House of Cards. Four corners and five places of business. That was because the Sohio and the Cards were both almost on top of one another. Cammy was listing everything for Andrew.

"Don't you think I can see?" he said.

"I'm just telling you," she answered. "There's the Art House Movies and Gallegher Drugs."

"Come on, Cammy. Just be quiet, I want to concentrate on what I can see."

"Well . . ." she began.

"Shhhh," he said. There was his kind of music on the radio again. It was slow and bluesy, with a woman singing about going out the door. Andrew was listening and studying his driving while scanning the sidewalks to see who was out before supper. He waved a few times. Girls.

They went on. Two churches, two filling stations, one drugstore, Cammy listed to herself, one bakery, a movie, a jewelry store called 68 Silver. A grocery called Cantrells. Something called Gormand-To-Go, Catering. Baum's Hardware. Starr Bank, and Carry-Out, Beer, Wine. We-Cash-Checks—Two I.D.'s.

"That's about it," Cammy said, as the last light changed and Andrew turned the truck toward home.

"Thanks for the riding," Cammy said, once they were parked. "I'm about dry now, too."

"Well, you could change your clothes if you wanted to," Andrew said. "Mom's home."

"Is it that late?" Cammy said, and then, "How'd you know?"

There wasn't a sign that anyone was home. "I can tell when a house has somebody in it," he said.

"No, you can't! You saw the light in the kitchen. You!" Cammy laughed and ran up on the porch, threw open the door and went running to the kitchen. Her mama was at the sink, cutting up vegetables. Her cup of tea was getting cold on the table.

"Cammy, if you jump on my back, I'll brain you."

"I wasn't going to!" Cammy laughed and gave her mama a big hug and kiss. "Ummmm, you smell good."

"Hi, Cam, sorry I can't say the same about you. Where you been?"

"Been with Andrew and . . ." She was about to say Richie but stopped herself. Didn't know how much her mama knew. "He took me for a ride."

Andrew came in and slumped in the chair at the kitchen table.

Cammy and Maylene faced him. Maylene had her back against the sink. Her hands were still wet from the vegetables. Cammy didn't care. She held onto them anyhow. Her mama wore her diamond engagement ring but not her wedding band. Her mama was so beautiful. Her hair came out around her shoulders like a big fan. It was dark, like her eyes. Cammy looked up at her. She smiled down at her daughter.

"You're so pretty," Cammy said. "Wish I could be pretty like you when I grow up."

Her mama snuggled her tightly in her arms.

"You look about a day older than Andrew," Cammy said.

"Had to be the longest day of my life," said Maylene.

Cammy laughed. "No, you could be my older sister and not my mom."

"That would sure be a topic of conversation," Andrew said, watching them. He had sat down at the table and was sipping Maylene's tea.

"How you doing, sport?" Cammy's mama said.

"Maylene, baby," he said.

"What you up to—gimme a hug," his mama said.

Andrew unfolded himself, like it pained him, from the chair. Came over and let Maylene give him a hug and a kiss. "My babies," she said.

"I'm not a baby," he said.

"Yes, you are, you'll always be my first baby," she said.

"I'll always be your first but not a *baby*," he said. "Not anymore."

"Um-hum," Maylene murmured, brushing her hand through his hair.

"Mom, come on, let go." They were real close. Cammy was being squeezed but she didn't mind. She grabbed her brother and held on. But finally, her mama let him go and so did she.

"So you took Cammy for a ride. Where?"

He was silent.

"Richie with you?"

Silence, again. Cammy said uh-huh before she could stop herself.

She kept her eyes on the floor.

"I just took him around to the auto plant so he could fill out an application," Andrew said.

"I'll say one thing for you, Andrew. You're a good cousin. You never give up on him. But he's not worth your effort," Maylene said.

"Don't say that, Mom. He can't help the way he is. If I had Aunt Effie for a mother, I'd be like that, too, I bet."

"Speaking of my sister." Before she turned back to her work at the sink, Maylene fixed her eyes on Cammy.

Oh, boy, Cammy thought.

Maylene was lean, not too tall. She had a good shape, Andrew said. Cammy liked her legs best. They had a good shape, too.

"My sister called me about one Cammy," Maylene said. Cammy knew right away that she'd better tell the truth because there was no telling what Aunt Effie had told. So she did tell it all the way it happened. By the time she finished she was crying. "She said mean things about Gram Tut," Cammy managed. "I mean, Patty Ann did. And she's just as crazy as she can be. Just upchucking every day! I hate all of them. I wish they'd all die."

"Cammy. You should have sympathy for your cousin. She's got real problems."

"They better just shut about Gram Tut," she said.

"Well, you could have been nicer to your cousin, Cam. And Effie did dry your clothes for you. But you had no business over there at the Care. You know they don't allow you there without an adult. It's not healthy, you hanging out at an old people's home," her mama said.

"Who says it's not?" Andrew said, defending Cammy. "Effie, probably, right?" he said. "I swear, Mom, sometimes I don't believe it's you. Cammy likes visiting Gram Tut, what's wrong with that? Don't let Effie influence you," he told Maylene.

"You know better than that," Maylene said. "I'm talking to Cammy."

"Yeah, well, Cammy's okay. She's the most sane kid I know. And sweet, and got her own mind, too. Don't you take Aunt Effie's side," he told Maylene.

Cammy felt like she would burst with love for her big brother. She went over and stood in front of him. She had her arms folded across her chest. She never was sure how long he would be nice to her. She stood and looked at him. He reached for her, took the top of her head in his hand and spun her around. It was just the nicest thing!

"I'm a top!" she said. He kept spinning her and she started giggling like crazy.

Finally, when she was dizzy, she knew she'd had enough. She fell on the floor, set there, moaning softly, "My head, oooh, Andrew. You about killed my head!"

And then, she didn't know why, but maybe she thought she was helping Andrew out of something. It just came to her and she told her mama.

"It wasn't Andrew at all," she began. "It was Richie with the bottles. Andrew wouldn't have any."

Her mother turned around from her work at the sink, as Andrew jumped to his feet.

"You stupid. . . !" Andrew began. He gritted his teeth and stood over his sister like he really was going to kill her.

"That's enough," Maylene said.

"I'll never take you anyplace again," Andrew said.

"Andrew," Maylene said.

"Don't talk to me. Don't come near me!" Andrew said.

"Andrew?" Cammy pleaded. "I was just . . ."

"Drop dead!" he said to her. Made her cry all at once. She sobbed there with her head on her knees, couldn't help it.

"That's right," Maylene said. "Defend a no-good and make your little sister cry."

"Don't talk about Richie!"

"I'll talk about him, I'll say the truth about him whenever I feel like it." Maylene said. "You fool around with him long enough and you'll end up just like him."

"Oh, man, that's just swell. I don't care if I end up like Richie. He's who he is. He doesn't pretend anything else."

"That's dumb, Andrew. I thought you were more intelligent than that."

"Well, I thought you at least would feel for someone who's got problems," Andrew said. "Where's your sympathy for your fellow man?"

Maylene was silent a moment. Cammy looked up now and wiped her eyes. "Don't fight," she said, almost in a whisper. They heard her but they weren't listening to her. Nobody ever did. "Wish I had my own radio," she said, wistfully. Maylene stared at her for a long moment.

She looked back at Andrew. "I have sympathy and give it where it belongs. There comes a point when a kid can't make excuses anymore."

"Yeah," Andrew said. "I'd say Aunt Effie is one good excuse."

"Yeah?" Maylene said. "And what's your excuse? If you're not with Richie, you're by yourself. You have an easy job through your dad that pays you more than you give."

"You really hate Dad, don't you?" Andrew said, softly.

"Oh, Andrew, I don't hate him. I know him, is all. I'm talking about what you should be doing for yourself. About getting your life together and going to college."

"Mom, I'm sixteen years old!"

"Sixteen, almost seventeen, graduating next year. With brains for college."

"Oh, so now Dad should send me to college. You know you won't give me any money for college."

"Thank you. And you know I haven't got anything extra from what I make."

"Mom, not everybody has to go to college."

"'A mind is a terrible thing to waste,'" Cammy chanted. Nobody heard.

"I don't want you to depend so on your father. He's here today but he may disappear on you tomorrow."

"That was you and him. That's not me and him," Andrew said.

Maylene looked down at the floor. Uneasily, she placed the flat of her hands on the side of the sink behind her.

"You guys stop it, please," Cammy pleaded. "Mama?" Cammy came over and put her arms around her mama's waist, her head on Maylene's side. "Don't fight, Mama."

Maylene ran her hands through Cammy's hair. "Am I your baby, too?" Cammy murmured.

But her mama stayed quiet, her mind on Andrew.

"Look, I don't want any supper," Andrew said. "I got to go for a while. I took the afternoon off from work and I got to make it up to Dad somehow."

"Andrew, stay long enough to eat your supper," Maylene said.

"I'm not hungry, really, Mom. I'll eat later."

"What's the point of my cooking?" she asked him. But he was going. He left.

"What about me? I'm here," Cammy said. "You have to cook for me, too."

Maylene sighed. "I know, baby. Don't you give me a hard time."

"Well, you forget all about me for Andrew."

"Cammy, you know that isn't true."

"You only worry about him."

"Cammy, please shut it. You have some answering to do to Aunt Effie. You worry me when you run off and do as you please."

"I didn't run off," she pleaded. "Mama, I just went to see my Gram."

Maylene sighed. "I don't know which is worst, having you roaming by yourself or having you stay with Andrew when he's driving Richie."

"I don't like it too much when Richie's with us," Cammy said.

"Did you just go out to the plant; did Andrew really leave him there?"

"Yes. He tried to get Richie in the line but he wouldn't go. Mama, there were oh, so many people—hundreds, Andrew said. Richie just laid down on the ground. And Andrew took his bottle away from him."

"What'd Andrew do with it?"

"Put it back in the pup, I think," Cammy said. "Mama? Andrew and me rode around. He didn't have a drink or anything. He was nice to me. He gave me a whole candy bar. That was when Richie—Mama?"

"What, baby."

"Why is it that my dad won't live with us?"

"You know, Cammy. He and I are divorced. Do you miss not having a father?"

"Well, I don't know," Cammy said. "Not like I miss Gram Tut." She squeezed her eyes shut tight but that didn't stop the tears.

"Cammy. Cammy, don't cry. Oh, you worry me so. Why can't you just come home after day camp and stay out of trouble?"

"Because there's nobody here!" she cried. "Andrew's at work!"

"But only for a couple of hours after you get home," Maylene said. "And you know how to come inside, fix yourself some peanut butter and just rest or watch TV."

"It's not the same," Cammy sobbed. "Gram Tut always had something special. Cookies, or doughnuts!"

"You know it's been years since she made stuff like that," her mama said.

"No, it hasn't been, either," Cammy whined. "Gram watched for me to come home. She just couldn't wait to see me and hug me, and feed me!"

Maylene held her daughter close. "Are you hungry, baby?"

"Yes! I'm starved."

"Okay. I'm making lamb chops."

"What else?" Cammy asked. She wiped her tears on her mama's front.

"Let's see. How about some fast baked potatoes in the microwave?"

"And brown 'em next to the lamb chops in the oven?" she knew the answer. "Andrew doesn't like lamb chops," Cammy said.

"Well, then, he can eat straw," her mama said.

"Ooh-hoo!" Cammy hooted. "He'll only eat chicken or spaghetti with meat sauce."

"You sound just like him," her mama said.

"Well, it's true," Cammy said.

"Well, can you imagine me cooking just chicken and spaghetti all week?"

"No," Cammy said. "But I like them both."

"Yes, but not all the time," Maylene said. And sighed.

"I bet Andrew went to take food to Richie," Cammy said. She did not tell her mama that after she went to work, Richie came over and had toast and coffee and slept on their couch most mornings. She swore to Andrew she wouldn't tell.

"Do you have any idea how exhausted I am right now?" Maylene asked her daughter.

Cammy leaned back to get a good look at her mama. She searched Maylene's face. There was her mama, as pretty as a picture. She wished she had eyes so big. Cammy had little eyes, just like her dad's, Andrew said. She saw her dad rarely. And since he didn't live in town, she didn't have to think about him, most of the time. She didn't see how anybody could leave somebody as pretty as her mama. Divorced.

She held her mama tight. Closed her eyes. Breathed in the familiar scent of her. All of a sudden, she just wanted to go to sleep right where she was. Take a good nap. What had her mama asked her? Exhausted?

"No," Cammy said. "Uhn-uh."

The Bluety

5 The way all the kids said the name made it sound like "L-O-D." Like, one, two, three, L-O-D. Cammy never knew to call her cousin anything but L-O-D, which, she found out in school, was spelled E-l-o-d-i-e, Elodie. She'd never stopped to think that cousin Elodie might have other names. Elodie was just Elodie, like Cammy was Cammy. That is, until a few months ago, when her mama said something about Elodie's name being Eloise Odie.

"That is a-a-mazing!" Cammy said. "I never knew that."

"You probably just forgot she carries her stepfather's last name," her mama said.

"I mean," Cammy went on, "here's somebody who's always one thing, like L-O-D, and will be forever, you think. And then, she turns out to be L-O-Weez, for goodness sakes!"

Her mama told her, "When you all start in dating and stuff, I bet L-O-D will become Eloise and you will be Camilla."

"Who'd want to call us those ugly names?" Cammy replied. "L-O-D is L-O-D, just like I am Cammy, and forever. When do we start in dating?"

Her mama laughed at that and said, "Oh, not for several years, at least."

But you had to wonder about parents, sometimes, Cammy was thinking now. She and Elodie were on the bus to day camp.

"With all the names in the world," she said to Elodie, "a kid's mom and dad have to go come up with the worst."

Elodie nodded. "A baby don't have a thing to say about it, too," she said.

"We are at their mercy," Cammy added. "I'm glad I only have a mom to worry about."

"That don't matter," Elodie told her. "You know where your dad is. You can see him if you want to. And you have all us cousins and aunts and uncles and stuff."

Poor Elodie. She had to make sure Cammy and her family included her in as a relative. Well, she really was, Cammy thought, even though she was a third cousin. She had been adopted by second cousin Marie Lewis Odie when she was seven weeks old. Third cousins weren't close in kinship, not like first cousins. But they were definitely in.

Wish Elodie could be as first as Patty Ann,

thought Cammy. She's more of a friend than *that* first cousin. Patty Ann was the only one of them with a decent name. All the girls thought Patricia Ann was a beautiful, rich-sounding name. It was so unfair!

Patty Ann sat up front next to this boy, Larry, but two seats behind Ms. Devine, the Crafts instructor. Ms. Devine sat behind Tim, the bus driver and camp helper. Cammy and Elodie sat five rows back on the right, where they could get a good view of Patty Ann's long braid down her back, which she could sit on whenever she wanted to.

They looked on with their faces full of regret. But they pretended that Patty Ann in all her glory didn't upset them.

Between them and Patty Ann and Larry and Ms. Devine were other boys and other girls. The bus was half the size of a regular school bus.

Cammy didn't know why she was thinking about names. Really, most of the time every other morning on the way to day camp, she didn't think about anything that could upset her. She would sit with Elodie and feel how wonderful was the morning in summer. It was swell to be up early and ready to begin all such grand things that were to happen. Such things came after Calisthenics and Crafts were over and after they'd gone for a walk, then rested about a half hour.

They would all load up again on the bus. They'd go to another part of the State Park, down dusty roads that were so hot, the air above them seemed to bend in the light. Mirages of water lay on the gravel roadbed. Everybody saw these pools of water that just faded once the bus got closer to them. Some kids said they saw Arab guys on horseback, whole caravans. And after they drove down the roads, they'd come upon the place.

It was a big, lone place in the sun and dust. Dark brown roofs, secretlike ways to the foot pool that had special water you walked through before entering the swimming pool. Shower stalls, lockers. Cool cement floors. Just wonderful. And last, the outdoor shower right before you hit the sun-hot concrete and jumped into this glorious, this sparkling pool, so big, it must've been built for giants, Cammy thought. Oh, it was just so great. They would even get swimming lessons from Miss Dayna, who looked like she just belonged in water. She was so bronze suntan, and oh, so long-legged and smooth in her swimsuit. But before this happened they'd eat their lunches after they'd changed into their bathing suits. And then they'd sing songs with Tim playing the guitar while their food rested up in their stomachs.

On the bus now, Cammy couldn't wait for all of it to happen like ABC. She couldn't wait especially for the lunch and swim part. She had the window seat. Always did. Elodie let her have her way about most things.

Let's see, thought Cammy. She wanted to recall

every minute of the morning. First, she got up and her mama had her knapsack all packed. Her lunch was in the refrig and Cammy made sure to take it up.

Got my swimsuit and my bathing cap rolled in my towel, she was thinking. And got my comb and brush for after the swim.

Everything was in her knapsack with her on the bus.

Left the house at eight-thirty. Locked the door, too. Left old Richie sleeping dead away on the living room floor.

Andrew hadn't let Richie sleep on the couch because Richie didn't look too clean. Richie didn't care. He'd slept in Andrew's pup most of the night, anyway. Cammy's mama left at seven-thirty and Richie had come in about eight. He must've seen Maylene's car pool ride leave.

That Richie. Said he put his name on the plant list, but Cammy didn't know. What if her mama found out he was staying with them in the house sometimes? Lordy.

She pushed away all worrisome thoughts. She had walked a mile to the Lawn where they started out for day camp. Lawn used to be this mansion place, her mama said. It was all painted white with green trimming, and with the biggest rooms, and a porch all the way around. No one lived in it now. But once, Mr. Harrison lived there. Now there were just offices belonging to the town in there.

They had sat on the Lawn porch and waited for the bus. Right in front of them was the flagpole with the American flag moving so gentle. Hardly a breeze.

I pledge a-lee-juhnce! And the sun was there on the side of the pole. And all of the kids and Cammy sat in the sunshine on the porch. All of them in shorts and tennis shoes, hair combed. They were all cleaned up for the day camp. The sky was all blue—still was—and the flagpole was about to poke it, it looked like. The girls were together and the boys were together on the veranda with just a little space between one side and the other.

Sometimes, one of us goes steady with a boy, Cammy thought. Mama says we don't "go" anyplace, except on the way to and from school, or to a party. Because we are too young, she says. But I don't know. Patty Ann goes with Larry Hughes all this week. Aunt Effie doesn't know it and would murder Patty Ann if she did. Aunt Effie says there best be a war-between-the-sexes until a girl gets a ring on her finger. "Never trust a man," she says, "until he pays for the wedding and the first year's rent."

Patty Ann and Larry had sat together coming home from day camp on Tuesday. Boys had teased them. Some mean stuff. "Watch out, Larry, she might upchuck in your face!" Stuff like that.

Larry jumped up, said stuff like, "Step outside. Step outside!" Just like some grown man about to fight, too.

Everybody laughed, because how do you step outside on a moving bus? That is, everybody laughed except Patty Ann.

Boys loved her face and her hair and her *attitude,* Mama called it. The way she "carried" herself. But the rest of her from the neck down was junk-and-sick. Patty Ann was real like a stick; she didn't stand up straight, either.

Elodie and me, we don't go with anyone right now, Cammy was thinking. But I like the day camp a lot. Some say it's lonely. That's because kids whose mamas work or ones who don't have mamas, or the ones who live at the Christian Shelter, are the only kind that come to day camp. And not your true friends.

Well, Aunt Effie didn't lift a finger; didn't have to get up to go to work because Uncle Earl had a fine job as a car salesman. She wasn't poor at all and let Patty Ann come. Wouldn't think somebody like Patty Ann would want to.

But I think she wants to get good and away from Aunt Effie, too, Cammy thought. I bet that's why she comes to camp.

Looking out the window on this day-camp day of Thursday. One more day-camp day this week and that will be Saturday. That's how Cammy was thinking, her thoughts moving with the bus. Thinking on wheels.

Cammy liked it that she could be alone by herself but, also, with Elodie whenever she wanted company. Elodie didn't mind when Cammy looked out the window and didn't talk. Cammy knew Elodie watched her closely, waiting for her to say something so she could jump in. Be friends. Or Elodie waited to tell her something, if and when Cammy got bored with looking out.

Oh, it was a swell day.

The bus went all the way downtown to get gas at the filling station. They were relaxed like passengers going to the Mall. Then it went all the way up the main street and then turned left. They got on Devil's Backbone, which was scary.

Kids called it the D-bone road. All shade and light making funny shapes, going on-off, light-dark as they went through trees on each side of the road.

All the windows were wide open. The breeze blew in Cammy's face, dried the sweat on her forehead and the wet of her hair behind her ears. It felt cool on her face after that. Cammy closed her eyes. She knew when Elodie leaned around to try to see her. She opened her eyes. "What is it, girl?" she said, none too kind.

"You going to sleep right here?" Elodie asked.

"I'm taking the breeze," Cammy said, "but if I feel like dozing off, I sure will." She wasn't sleepy. But she did want to be left alone.

"If I come home with you after day camp, we can play or something?" Elodie said.

"Girl, don't bother me about when-we-come-home. We haven't even started, yet."

Elodie set back in her seat. She knew Cammy didn't want her over. But always, she tried asking.

Cammy felt funny about it each time Elodie asked to come home with her. Felt funny about saying no. She didn't want people seeing her with Elodie, that was her deep, dark secret. She was ashamed of it. But she was more ashamed of Elodie.

She's poor, Cammy thought and felt ashamed, thinking. Has to live at the Christian Shelter a lot, in the summer, like now. With her mom up by the lakes on a crew doing the migrant work.

They let Elodie stay for day camp. Cammy didn't know who "they" were, exactly. But her mama said that "they" paid for Elodie. Because cousin Marie didn't have the money to send her to camp, but didn't want Elodie up there with her, either. North, by the lakes, where the crew lived practically in the fields from sunup until almost night.

"They" paid for it and helped the family so Elodie wouldn't have to migrant labor, Cammy was thinking.

"It's a good town," Cammy's mama said often enough. Had a good Care for Cammy's Gram. And kindness for the less fortunate, like Elodie.

So I should be nice to her, Cammy thought. I know that! But what will other kids think if she comes to my house? Richie's enough trouble!

Cammy fidgeted. It's not right to feel bad about Elodie because she's poor and near homeless. But kids will tease me. They see me playing with her in my own yard. I could say I just ran into her downtown, or something.

It's different at day camp, Cammy thought. Me

and Patty Ann are the best here because we have houses to live in and good stuff at home. She's got better stuff than I have. She has nice clothes.

It's okay to be kind to kids that are worse off.

Oh, I hate all about it!

She sighed. She turned to Elodie, who was sitting there not looking out or anything. She stared straight ahead. Cammy was just about ready to invite her home after day camp today when Elodie nodded toward Patty Ann and Larry.

Cammy looked. Larry had his arm across the back of the seat. He was playing with Patty Ann's long, pretty braid. Then, he twisted and untwisted it around his hand, gently pulled it. The pulling made Patty Ann's head jerk back a little each time. Larry was turned toward her, looking down at her face. Patty Ann leaned toward him. Just a little. Elodie and Cammy could see she was grinning all over herself.

Her face, what they could see of it, looked dreamy.

"They make me sick," Cammy whispered to Elodie. Elodie didn't say anything. She wrung her hands in her lap; laced and unlaced her fingers.

"You still crazy about Larry?" Cammy asked her. She tried to speak kindly.

Elodie nodded. She didn't look up.

"Well, he's too old," Cammy said. "He's almost thirteen. I mean, he's twelve," she whispered, "but anybody that old shouldn't be going to day camp when some of the kids on this bus aren't but ten."

Elodie looked about to say something. But instead, she shrugged. Her eyes were misty. She was sure still in love, thought Cammy.

"Listen. You can come over after day camp," she said. "But I have to go see my Gram Tut before we can play."

"That's okay with me. I always did like Gram Tut," said Elodie.

Well, she's not *your* Gram, Cammy thought. She didn't say it. Oh, it was hard, always thinking about other people's feelings. Her mama said she was different from most children by the way she cared about other people's feelings.

Wish I didn't, Cammy thought. Wish I could be just hard as nails like some people I know.

She looked at Patty Ann. Cammy felt hard as nails inside toward her one second. The next second, she felt peevish that she wasn't more like her.

Why wasn't I made that pretty? she wondered. Why does she have everything and I don't? Good in school, and I am good only sometimes, not in everything. Knows how to say things to the teachers that they like. And can sit just as still in Assembly when it is all so pitiful! Me and Elodie have to slump down and poke each other. Like the rest of the kids, and cause a commotion. Not Patty Ann!

Don't think about it. Oh, look out the window. Oh, look! We're off the D-bone already. We're climbing the steep road up to the State Park. Oh, it about drives me crazy that it takes so long. But we are up and up, soon. We go around the school forest. Kids planted all the trees there for at least the last seventy-five years, Mama says. Whew! That's a lo-oo-ong time!

Cammy looked over into the pine forest as they went by. She could see some of it, the paths where the trees were cut and dragged out at Christmastime.

Everybody in town came up to get a Christmas tree and have hot chocolate. Her mama said it was a swell tradition, the Christmas tree-cutting at the school pine forest.

You can see our town—Mama says its no more than a village. If you are a town, you have to have a jail! But you can see our "town" way off on another hill from where the bus goes by, Cammy thought. She caught a glimpse of it just now.

She leaned back to watch as the gravel road changed to a dark, pavement road. And they were in the State Park. Wood signs, direction arrows carved in the wood. Upper Level, Lower Level.

Old coach road to Cincinnati. Parking, Lower Level.

There's the sign I want! Oh, great! Shelter, Lower Level. That's us! Cammy thought, excitedly.

"It's so fun, the first thing in the morning," she said to Elodie.

"Yeah, it is," Elodie answered. She was close behind Cammy's back. Cammy leaned against her. Elodie rested her chin on Cammy's shoulder. For a moment, they were just like sisters, looking, feeling the same and seeing the same.

"I can't wait!" Cammy said. "You know what I mean?"

"Yeah, me neither," Elodie said. They both straightened up and turned facing front.

The bus pulled into a parking space. They all grabbed their belongings and headed for the stone and wood shelter. It was open all around for four feet above the stone walls. The roof was dark brown like the trim. The shelter was large and roomy, with long tables, a standing grill in the center and a big, old fireplace at one end. You had to sign up for the shelter.

Our day camp has it for three mornings a week, Cammy thought.

"Line your lunches on the table," said Ms. Devine, as they went inside the shelter.

The counselor for the day camp met them there. He was John Blockson. Mr. Blockson had the kids write their names on slips of paper and pin the papers to their swim-towel rolls. These were then stowed in duffel bags. Next, their lunches were stacked in a kind of rolling locker. Tim took the duffels and locker on a wagon to stow in the baggage part of the bus.

Cammy was so excited! The duffels with their lunches and swim clothes would go to the next stop and be waiting for them at lunchtime.

When Tim came back, he blew his whistle. No need to tell the campers. They all lined up on the open grass behind the shelter. The dew was still dampening the ground and wetting their sneakers.

"Calisthenics," said Mr. Blockson. Tim helped him lead, bending deeply where the counselor couldn't.

They went through their routines to music from a tape player with a small loudspeaker. Oh, they sure could exercise to music. The girls tried to make it almost a dance, knee bends and stretches, side bends and leg lifts. The boys tried to be cool, almost break-dancing, it seemed like. Everybody was grinning. Even laughing. Ms. Devine sat on a picnic table just kind of smiling in the sunlight. It wasn't her turn to work them yet. She was too big to move fast. Once in a great while, she would do the exercises.

They were all breathing hard after a half an hour. But, oh, the fresh air! thought Cammy.

"Did you see how Patty Ann had to set down not even halfway through?" asked Elodie. They were sitting in the shade at a picnic table. They rested while finishing up the cornhusk dolls they'd learned to make last week.

"I don't care," Cammy said. "She gets tired quick, I guess," she said.

"And wearing those shorts," Elodie went on. "They look about to fall off to her feet—no hips."

"L-O-D, I don't *care*. Let's just forget her," Cammy said.

They did forget Patty Ann, or tried to. But she

always caught their attention. There she was, she and Larry with some kids at the next picnic table. All of them in shade but Patty Ann. She was in light and shade. The light caught strands of her hair. Her hair framed her face in waves rippling into that perfect French braid down her back. The waves shone like copper. So did her lashes. She looked like a princess.

And the whole park must be her daddy's kingdom, Cammy thought. Oh, I don't care!

Until Ms. Devine had to go and use Patty Ann to show them stuff.

"Students," said Ms. Devine. "If you will stop a moment and see what Patty Ann is doing. Children! Patty Ann, stand up and show your doll. Now some of you are having trouble with the arms. Show them, dear, how to take the shuck and wrap it around one arm. See, she forms the sleeve starting somewhere around a fourth inch from the hand of the arm. She wraps it up toward the head— see? Now some of you have had trouble with getting the head tight enough. Patty Ann will go around and show you all who are having trouble. Some of you boys with your boy dolls need to pay attention."

Cammy liked Ms. Devine fine, until she had to let Patty Ann show them stuff. Andrew once told Cammy that what Patty Ann was about was some "self-filling profit," it sounded like he said. Since everybody knew Patty Ann was good in school, she got to be the leader of things just on general principles. And because she was made the leader, she thought she was one, too, and would be good in school because it was expected of her.

But what was wrong with making the kind of doll you wanted? Cammy thought suddenly. I mean, I wet the husk for five minutes like Ms. Devine says to. But I want my doll to be like I want it and not the way she says it ought to be.

Cammy stuck her lip out and did it her way. She liked her doll's head to look more round than square. She wanted the arms to be longer and clasped in front, not sticking out to the sides. The whole thing made her fed up with Patty Ann.

When she came around to their table, Patty Ann acted real nice. She didn't look at Cammy. But she smiled down at Elodie. She took Elodie's doll into her hands. You could hardly see her hands work over it, but you could see the doll change into something really good. Right before Cammy's eyes, too.

"Well, I'll be," said Elodie. She looked up at Patty Ann as if Patty Ann were some kind of queen. "Can I come sit beside you to do her hair?" Elodie asked.

"I know how to do the hair, look at mine," Cammy told her. She had her doll's hair almost done. She tied the dampened cornsilks around her dolly's forehead with the string, then flipped back the cornsilks so the face would show and the string would be hidden under the hairline. It was nice that cornsilk hair could be blond, or reddish or dark brown, depending on when it was stripped off the corn.

But Elodie pretended she didn't hear Cammy.

"Sure, you can come sit by me," Patty Ann told Elodie.

Elodie got up, left Cammy's side to sit with Patty Ann. Cammy couldn't believe it. It was like Elodie forgot how she felt about Patty Ann. Forgot how they both felt about her.

Elodie settled down on one side of Patty Ann, who had Larry on her other side. And then, Larry started being nice to Elodie, since Patty Ann was. It was as if all of a sudden the three of them were best friends. All at once, Elodie had become popular. Everyone else at the table over there began to notice Elodie. "See my doll, ain't it cute?" somebody said to her.

Cammy pretended she was deaf, busy with her doll.

"Elodie, your doll's hair is the same shade as mine is."

Cammy could've cried. I don't care! Who cares? she thought.

But it felt like suffering forever, being left out the way she was. There were only two other people at her table, both boys and both nerds. Well, there was Esther Lovejoy, who was also at the table. She didn't count. She was near raggedy and they say she had lice sometimes. When you lifted her hair in back, her neck was dark gray, it was so dirty. Cammy had seen it once. And here she was by herself, with Esther of the pale fish eyes across the table from her. Just because Patty Ann stole Elodie away.

6 🍃 It was an agonizing time before the doll-making was over. Cammy made her way through it, feeling awful inside. But before it was over, Elodie got what was coming to her, too. Patty Ann lost interest in her, or forgot that she was paying Cammy back for the other day, when Cammy was over there during the rainstorm. When Cammy said bad stuff to Patty Ann and ran away from Aunt Effie, too.

Patty Ann got back at Cammy and then she and Larry just up and left Elodie. And then, everybody at that table shied away from Ms. Eloise Odie.

Cammy watched it all. Larry and Patty Ann finished their dolls first. Then everybody else finished, except Elodie, who sat there looking like somebody had stolen her heart and then cut it up and ate it. Big eyes, all misty and sad. Cammy almost felt sorry for her, but not quite. Elodie turned around and looked over at Cammy. Cammy stared right back. She smirked. But then, she turned away.

Elodie did come back to Cammy's table. Too late. They weren't quite friends anymore but they would probably play together.

"Can I still come over after camp? Remember, you said I could," Elodie had the guts to ask.

Kid, you've got a lot of nerve! Cammy should've said, but she didn't. She was still too mad, and upset, she had to admit. "Should of thought about that before," was what she managed to say without her voice trembling.

Elodie's eyes brimmed with tears. Then the tears kind of sank back.

Cammy let her stew. Maybe she would let her come on over. Maybe she wouldn't. Nothing said she had to tell just now, so she didn't.

And then, things happened, one after the other, the way they always did at camp. Just regular like ABC. They finished their dolls. Each was given a sack to put each one in with the owner's name on it. They were told to take them home to show the dolls to their parents. It was nice to have a doll for the table way on to Thanksgiving time. Cammy smelled the air, to see if she could smell cold Thanksgiving coming. She couldn't. It was still late August. Still hot and steamy.

They went for their nature walk. Ms. Devine always went with them. She was the last one, because she was so big and slow. Sometimes, the helper, Tim, who had been in college but quit, came a little later.

"Let's go *down*!" kids shouted. "Yeah! Yeah! Let's do!"

"Too far, you won't feel like swimming after," said Ms. Devine.

"No it's not! We need a good walk. We need to skip rocks! Ooh, yeah!"

"She just doesn't feel like moving herself down that far," Cammy murmured to no one in particular.

Elodie was right there, grinning in her face.

"Step aside, kid," Cammy said. She didn't care if she did hurt Elodie's feelings. This was her walk. She could pretend she was by herself, if only Ms. Devine would let them go down.

"I will let you if you listen to me good," Ms. Devine was telling them. "Now I don't want any roughhouse from you boys—Larry."

"Me-ee?" Larry said back, looking wounded. "I never do nothing and I always get the blame."

Everybody laughed. It was true in a way. Larry was too big a noise to do anything out-and-out. What he might do was to trip a kid on the path down and then pretend innocence. They all knew to look out for him, trip him up before he could start in. If you got him to his knees at first, everybody could use him to lean on as they went down.

Pretty soon, he was grinning because of the attention and allowed himself to be a good post to lean on.

Things happened, one after another all right. But what Cammy never knew was how fast they could change. Like a storm out in the country could come from nowhere. Its lightning would catch a house afire right before your eyes. Or a day that was all blue sky could turn over dark and dangerous while she was playing a game with the other campers, or just sitting on a bench. It could happen that fast. Change.

Funny how it is when we go down, Cammy thought. Pretty steep and with loose dirt and stones. Broken roots and such. Expect somebody will fall, hope it won't be me. Maybe it'll be Ms. Devine. Not for her to get hurt, Cammy thought. But for excitement. So I can tell Mama and Andrew how she fell down head first. So her head was downhill and her feet, uphill. And me and Patty Ann run to get help while Elodie guards big ole Ms. Devine.

Or maybe it's Patty Ann who falls. Skins her knees and twists her ankle. Blood all over her little pink socks. I have this white hanky to mop it up. Patty Ann rests her head on my shoulder, too. "You just hold still," what I tell her. "It'll stop bleeding in a minute. L-O-D, call 9-1-1."

Only, none of it happened. Nobody had fallen. Cammy guessed that was good. Most of them could almost run some of the way, slipping and sliding down the path of this slanty hillside. It was amazing that they still had to go down when you thought about being down on the lower level of the park to begin with. But the whole place was ridges and gorges, almost canyons, Andrew said, some of the ridges were so close and came down so far. Andrew said that you never thought about the midwest having canyons but it did sometimes—places in Illinois, too.

They went down to the Little River, that was its real name, which they all loved. Maybe because here the river was so swift sometimes. The Little swirled out toward this one place in the middle where the waters were still. Out there was an odd bluish color. Kind of sickly, and dark bluish-green. But mostly it was a blue mystery. Oh, so many stories about that blue place!

Andrew called it the blue hole. Mama said it had been there forever and was bottomless. She called it the blue devil. All the kids Cammy's age called it the bluety.

"There's the bluety!" somebody shouted.

That made them pause. Cammy felt a stripe of cold go through her at the name, the bluety. She knew all about it but now was no time to think on that. She had to get *down*.

Elodie was the first one down. She was so quick and nimble. Maybe she felt she should try harder because she was adopted, or something. But she always could go faster than almost anybody. Elodie didn't slide or trip or anything.

"There's the bluety! I kid you not, tooty!" It was Elodie making a rhyme and hollering up at them all still coming down. She was jumping this way and that, like she was fit to be tied.

Well, there were bushes, small trees that they clung to for balance, going down. Cammy couldn't see the bluety yet. It was exciting, that dark, deep place, but it wasn't her kind of thing, truly. Swimming pools were her personal favorite places. She could float on her back better than anything else. She would be a swell backstroker one day, her mama said.

Cammy saw the water of the Little River racing by. It seemed higher than usual. Muddy, close in. Some days, you could see bottom close to shore.

Not today, I bet, Cammy thought. Carefully, she made her way down, surprised to see that her sneakers were mudcaked.

Bet the Little's been up as high as I am! So much rain, she thought.

She could see now. There wasn't any bank left, the Little was that far up.

No two ways about it. When she came off the slant, she would be in the water. So would everybody else, when they got to where she was. Did Ms. Devine know?

Elodie was off the hill and she was in the water, right at the Little's edge where it met the bottom of the hillside. In a second, her sneakers with her socks stuffed inside came flying up the slant. Cammy could see Elodie's face full of mischief.

You know you aren't to wade in the water! Cammy thought to tell her. But why tell Elodie anything?

One thing came after another, like counting out a deck of cards on a card table.

"Awh, L-O-D, watch what you're doing. You see what she did?" one kid complained. "Almost got me in the mouf' with her sneaker, too!"

"Yu-uk, Ucky!" somebody else said. The crowd coming down giggled and laughed.

One of Elodie's sneakers had hit the ground wrong; it bounced off and fell back down, turning over right into the water. Everybody hollered.

"Ooh-ooh, L-O-D!" kids hooted.

Kids were just being funny on a good day.

Couldn't see for looking, was what came to Cammy long after.

But things began to turn in a great circle.

Ms. Devine was way up above them. They could hear her panting. But she hollered down all of a sudden: "Now, L-O-D. Hon, stay still. Stay where you are." Panting hard, "Wait. L-O-D? L-O-D!"

Until Cammy thought she would hear the sound of Elodie's name in Ms. Devine's voice forever; probably would, too. And seeing that sneaker hit the water. They all did see it.

"L-O-D, wait for us! Wait for me!" It was Patty Ann calling L-O-D.

Well, can you believe that? Cammy thought.

Patty Ann took these giant steps right by Cammy. She must've wanted to wade in the water with Elodie or be first in right after her.

Cammy eased down, holding onto a bush. There wasn't anywhere to stand on flat land at the bottom without getting her feet into the water. She was thinking about that when Patty Ann went by, Larry on her heels.

"Better watch out," he told Cammy, as he passed.

"You little wimp, better watch out for *me,* too!" Cammy said under her breath. Larry turned around slowly, not missing a step. Just like he heard her. The look he gave her was the I'll-get-you-later-girl kind of look. Cammy didn't care.

"L-O-D, wait for me!" Cammy called, all of a sudden. She could hear meanness, get-evenness, in her voice. But that was for Patty Ann and Larry.

Elodie's my cousin, too, she thought. Patty Ann, you're not taking her away! She's *my* friend!

It was like a dream, her fighting for Elodie.

But none of them had seen the meaning in Elodie's sneaker falling. They'd all seen it roll down into the water, which had been really funny. Losing a sneaker in the Little River! That was something for Cammy to tell her mama and Andrew. How was Elodie going to get home with just one shoe?

She'd probably hop all the way, too, Cammy thought.

But Elodie recovered the sneaker and threw it up again only to have it fall back down into the water.

This time, the kids didn't have time to laugh. Cammy saw Elodie standing a few feet now from where the sneaker hit the river a second time. The sneaker filled with water. Sinking, it was moving away from Elodie.

Everything seemed still in the daylight. There was the river without a bank and where would they all stand? Cammy was thinking.

From that moment, she didn't remember moving for a long time. She watched as Elodie reached for her sneaker, and missed it.

Something caught hold of it, swirled it farther out. It went under. Elodie leaped to get her shoe. She jumped up and over, kind of, like a little kangaroo, or something. Both little paws, reaching out.

Kid. Kid, Cammy thought.

"L-O-D!" Ms. Devine, calling. "L-O-D!"

The call sounded weird now. Ms. Devine seemed to be calling through her teeth.

There was noise. Cammy didn't know what it was. She thought, wildly, bear. She could hear thrashing, a huge sound, coming down on her. She bent low and held to a bush, where she'd been for a long time. The noise was enormous, breaking away. It hurtled past her.

Ms. Devine. She hit the water, out of control. She scrambled back to the slant.

All of it was like a picture wheeling, to Cammy. For the first time, she saw it all. Ms. Devine, covered in mud and wet, scrambling out of the water. Elodie, sort of going backward in the water. She was making a big kind of U-turn. She'd tried for her sneaker and failed. Her face was just full of something, Cammy couldn't be sure what it was.

Fright, that's what it is.

Elodie's eyes, staring, pleading. They gleamed, searching for a friend.

Elodie!

Right on that, in one instant, Cammy knew Elodie was caught in the river. She saw it all.

Patty Ann. Larry was just off the hill, ankle-deep in water, holding his head. Seemed he was yelling. There was noise from lots of kids now.

Patty Ann. She'd left Larry behind. Went wading out toward Elodie. Her little hands were daintily up by her shoulders, as if to keep them dry. Then, she reached out toward Elodie.

They all could see the back of Patty Ann's head, her long hair riding like a tail on the water before it got too heavy. Patty Ann wasn't making a sound.

Elodie stared into her face. Cammy saw that, saw it all, like a spiraling in light.

Ms. Devine, trying to keep out of the water. Larry, jumping up and down, holding his head.

There were these loud sounds, coming from him—
"No! Look! Look! No! No!"

Patty Ann, wading out, moving in slow, long
strides in the water, her arms out. Going deeper;
then, getting carried closer to Elodie. Elodie reaching for her. Both, reaching.

All the time, the current was swirling in an arc
from near the hillside and pulling back into the
river. Curving like a big teardrop.

The bluety.

Oh. Oh. Cammy closed her eyes. There was
screaming now, all around her. Kids were scrambling back up the hillside. Ms. Devine was below
Cammy, holding onto the hill's bushes with her feet
in the water. Her voice was shrill, calling both Patty
Ann and Elodie.

Patty Ann and Elodie reached each other.
Cammy didn't know she had opened her eyes.
There was this look of peace all over Elodie's face.
It was just so swell, to see her face seem to break
out in happiness, with tears. Elodie was crying.

Cammy didn't know what Patty Ann was saying.
But she was sure Patty Ann was talking calmly to
Elodie. Elodie turned over on her back. Her head
pointed toward the hillside. Patty Ann had Elodie
under one arm. She guided her back toward the hill.
Patty Ann's left arm pushed through the water
while she kicked with her feet.

Cammy watched it all. She kept losing sight of it
in a daze. It was as if her eyes were closed and she

couldn't see. And yet, they were open the whole time. She felt she was actually using her own energy to help Patty Ann and Elodie. She could see Patty Ann's face now. That no-nonsense look as Patty Ann tried to bring Elodie out of the current. Elodie kicked her legs, helping. And they were more than halfway back now.

Cammy couldn't believe her cousin was so good at everything, and so brave. It made her feel proud. Yes!

Screams and cries, still loud all around. She saw when the current seemed to tug at them, seemed to jolt them. Was it swifter, coming back?

All at once, the sure look left Patty Ann. Never strong to begin with, now she seemed tired. The current had picked up, pulling both girls backward toward the bluety as they struggled forward. Patty Ann looked confused and hurt.

I won't get an A this time, her look seemed to say.

Cammy wanted to close her eyes. But she couldn't not look. Her mouth opened and she was crying out, she couldn't help it.

"Patty Ann! Patty Ann, hurry!"

Patty Ann gathered Elodie to her. Elodie was on her stomach now, struggling, terrified. She paddled furiously to get to safety. Patty Ann had her hands on Elodie's lower back. Both girls were going to be pulled into the swirling around the bluety.

But then, Patty Ann had her special expression

again, the kind that made folks say she was the best. That made people not notice that the rest of her was skin and bones. Her face was just perfect, like nothing Cammy had ever seen.

Patty Ann grabbed hold of Elodie. She was yelling something at Elodie. Then, Elodie surged halfway out of the water. At once helping her, Patty Ann gave her a real strong lift. Patty Ann's cheeks turned red as fire. Her legs churned furiously. Her face was twisted with the strain. She groaned a huge sound and pitched Elodie as far as she could. Kicked Elodie's behind straight toward the hillside, as Elodie leaped toward the land. All of it done in this suffering, bursting effort from Patty Ann.

Cammy saw it all as her eyes closed, opened, she couldn't tell. But she was seeing, and praying that she wasn't. Elodie, paddling for dear life. She did reach the hill, but the current carried her way down from where all of them were clinging to the slant. They could see her dig her hands into the hillside. Hands like claws. Cammy thought she could hear Elodie breathing, holding on. Too spent to yell or even cry.

Safe! Home! Don't move a muscle, Elodie. Hold tight! That was all Cammy could think about. Fastening the thought to her cousin with imaginary safety pins.

Hold tight, Elodie! Everything else, out of sight, out of mind.

When Cammy remembered, or stopped making herself forget about what could happen next, she looked. She couldn't see it. But it happened. It became part of the spinning wheel of sky and hillside, kids and blinding sunlight in her head, with no luck to it.

A silence came over everything. It pinned this day to them forever after. And Cammy to Patty Ann.

Beautiful Patricia Ann. All alone.

Her cousin.

The bluety.

Not a trace.

I Get It

7 Cammy woke up, slippery with sweat. She was breathing so hard, her chest ached. Her mama, Maylene, had to come in, comfort her, and that made her feel ashamed. During the night, Cammy could barely swallow. Her throat was raw from her screaming.

Her mama had to come in most nights. But then Andrew brought a cot and set it there right inside the doorway, about three feet from her bed.

"You just go to sleep," he told her. "And when I'm ready for bed, I'll come in and sleep on the cot awhile, to keep you company, so Mom can get some sleep, too. Okay, Cam?"

"Okay, Andrew," she said. Waves of cold came over her, made her voice waver. But she was so hoarse all the time, she could hardly get a sound out.

So Andrew did come in, to protect her, was the way she saw it. She slept most of the night, too. But somehow, she knew when he got up to go back to his room and his own comfortable bed. She was awake, or thought she was. Andrew wasn't there. Patty Ann was.

Sitting on the cot, looking at her. That smooth face so full of beauty. Patty Ann. Not dressed in her day-camp clothes the way she had been that fateful time of no luck anywhere. But wearing something fine. Something that was more than any color, in Cammy's mind. It was just so rich and beautiful, was all.

"Oh, Mama. Oh, Mama," Cammy moaned. She was scared out of her mind and commenced crying as if she'd never stop.

Patty Ann spoke to her. That made the darkness break into pieces. Cammy screamed. She came out of it when Andrew shook her and her mama put cold, wet dish towels across her forehead. Her brother and her mama talked softly and said kind things to her.

"Nothing's going to hurt you. I love you," Maylene told her, "Please, baby, don't take on so," holding her against the dark.

"Cam, you're not to blame for anything. It's not your fault, none of it," her big brother said. He squeezed her hand tight. Leaning toward her, Andrew sat on the cot right where Patty Ann had been.

But none of the night terrors happened right after that last, awful, Little River day. Right after was a week when there were church prayers and sadness in the town. But still, she got ready for school. New clothes and school supplies purchased at the Mall. And then, she went to school like everybody else. The day campers were happy to have been part of the "tragic event of late August," as the principal, Mr. Hardell, said. Cammy and her camp mates were stared at and talked about. At first, even Elodie was sought out by other children.

"I bet I told about it twenty times today," Cammy said to Andrew when she got home. "I'll see somebody coming my way, and it all just comes out, too."

"Don't upset yourself, Cam," he said. He had looked so serious.

"I don't feel anything about it, one way or the other," she said, airily.

Andrew had seemed worried about her, she didn't know why.

But things built up and fell down on her. The worst of anything was having to sit and see that desk. Each kid in homeroom had to bring a streamer of crepe paper. The teacher said it could be any color, as long as it was pastel. Soft colors, like pink or baby blue, even yellow. If a kid had a mind to bring in purple, well, it had to be a real pale purple. Cammy wouldn't know where to get a pale purple, anyway. Ms. Wells, the teacher, said she'd contribute the black crepe streamers to make the border.

So the way it was, Cammy got a roll of white crepe paper from the variety store. That had been all they had. She had most of the roll left over because she only needed one long strip. She wondered what she would do with it all.

I'll wind it around my neck and pin myself to the donkey with it, she thought, and then wondered why she'd thought that. She didn't feel right, though, somehow, inside.

But she had to admit Patty Ann's desk did look well decorated when they had finished it. Patricia Ann! When they'd all done it just as Ms. Wells directed them, it looked out of this world, Cammy thought.

"Just like Jesus might sit there," Elodie said. Cammy wished she'd thought to say that, even though kids snickered and looked mean at Elodie. Because all the kids agreed even if they wouldn't say so. Cammy could tell they did. The desk was now a sacred place. It scared them a little because they knew nothing on earth was good enough to sit in the seat with its black, black border.

The desk looked heavenly. It was like a prayer— *if I should die before I wake*—from all the children. None in Patty Ann's class had attended the real memorial service.

Yet, having to see the empty, decorated space all the time made Cammy's head start to hurt. After a couple of days, lots of kids got sick to their stomachs. Maybe it was the flu flitting from one to the next one of them. Maybe it wasn't.

Cammy stayed home sometimes. "I can't take school," she told her mama. "My tummy just turns over and up and down."

Andrew and her mama gave one another long looks, it seemed to Cammy. But she had to keep her eyes closed a lot of the time. Her head wouldn't stop aching. It felt like it was going to float off by itself. And it seemed as if she looked through a cloud when she tried watching TV.

Her mama took off from work half days to be at home with her. One time, Maylene also made a trip to school. She came home and told Andrew about it. Cammy had been lying on the couch with her bedspread over her and heard the whole thing.

"Why, the idea of it!" her mama said. "I told them, Patricia Ann's desk shouldn't be made into a centerpiece for a costume party, like some carved Halloween pumpkin. And the little kids sitting around all dressed up and having punch and cookies. Staring at that desk. Can you believe it? No wonder they're all getting sick. And it's ten days after the fact.

"Helen Wells told me Effie Lee was there, too, today," her mama told Andrew. "Said my sister thought it was real kind of the children to do such a thing. Considering none of them attempted to save her beloved child when doing something special and brave might've meant something, Helen said Effie said. Said my sister had a few choice words for the one adult who had been present that day. And she, of course, would be Ms. Devine, Helen said.

"They say Ms. Devine is leaving town." Maylene's voice sounded less angry now and more serious. Saying that folks had made it so uncomfortable for Ms. Devine. They talked about her being big and fat. "They called her a coward for not ever even trying to reach Patricia Ann, herself," her mama said.

Cold jitters jumped along Cammy's shoulders and down her spine. She felt Patty Ann come up close to the couch.

"They were calling Joyce Devine a fool, and worse, over the phone late at night," her mama said, "for allowing those children to go near that swollen Little River in the first place."

Then, things started getting worse and worse for Cammy. She had thought that the new school year, with new clothes and all, would be just cool for her. Yet, things went very wrong for her. But not as wrong as they went for Eloise Odie.

Naturally, everybody's meanness slowly came to rest on Elodie, who Patty Ann had saved. Elodie kind of shriveled up after she and Cammy and their classmates decorated Patty Ann's desk. When Cammy did manage to come to school once in a while, she could tell Elodie had really changed.

She always was a strange kid, anyway, Cammy

thought. But now, Elodie had stopped eating. Her face went blank and gray. She lost a lot of weight; she looked skinny, like Patty Ann had. She walked around in a weakened state. And she was all bent over, just like Patty Ann had been.

Kids said the ghost of Patty Ann visited Elodie one night and got inside her. Kids wouldn't talk to her anymore, wouldn't sit near her. They ran away every time she got close to them. Ms. Wells had a time. Kids would scream and vomit when Elodie came into class.

Cammy didn't know what it was nor how to stop it. But she, too, got sick to her stomach every time she looked at Elodie. She went home and stayed there.

Patty Ann started coming to Cammy's room at night. *"Hi, enemy."* Made Cammy scream. She knew Patty Ann was trying to get inside her, too.

"Effie is just the worst for keeping the children riled up," Maylene said. "Hollering and fainting and all, and tearing her hair in public. She won't let it alone."

They were in the kitchen. Even though it was hot late fall now, her mama had wrapped Cammy in a blanket because Cammy said she was cold all over. She did feel cold, too, her mama commented.

Cammy was draped across her mama's lap. Her head rested on Maylene's shoulder; her face was buried in her neck.

Andrew was there. He always was at evening

time, since she had been sick. "She came in, making sure the desk was still decorated and it's been more than three weeks," Andrew said. Talking about Aunt Effie. "She always manages to come when Ms. Wells is in the teachers' room for her lunch. Just walks into the school."

"Well, they'd better start locking the doors against her, if they want the children to stop being hysterical," Maylene said. "Anyway, they shouldn't leave the school wide open the way they do. The way the world is, anything could happen."

Her mama and Andrew thought Cammy was asleep. They talked quietly, so as not to disturb her. She knew this. And she was either asleep or awake or in between. Most of the time, she was in between, feverish.

"Anyway," her mama said, "it was my own sister, Effie Lee, who started that awful business about her Patricia Ann's ghost walking inside L-O-D."

Words came and went in puffs of sweet powder. One of the puffs was written, "Walking inside me." Cammy moaned with its aching.

"I never wanted her to die."

"Hush, baby."

"Did I say that?"

"Yes, but hush. Nobody blames you."

Moaning, "They blamed L-O-D."

"That poor, poor child. As though not having a family wasn't enough. Then she has to get saved by the most loved and envied child in town, who gets drowned herself."

Cammy didn't know how she found out. She felt always in a dream. And in the dream, Elodie was moving out of town. Elodie's mom came and got her and Elodie would have to migrant labor in the camps with her mother. She wouldn't stay at the Christian Shelter anymore. It wasn't a dream at all. It was real.

"Awful," her mama said. "Lord, if I could take her in, I would. But I don't think it would do Cammy any good. That would just bring it all back."

"It hasn't ever gone away," Andrew said. "If Cammy could just remember seeing Patty go down, I think that would complete it."

"Do you, Andrew?"

"Sure. If she could admit she saw her cousin drown, then she could admit Patty was really gone forever."

"I never saw it! I didn't. I didn't!"

"It's okay, Cam, seeing it doesn't make you guilty."

"I never saw. I never, I don't remember!"

"'Drew, leave her alone about it," someone said.

"What? Who's that?"

"Cam, it's our dad come to see you."

And then, a long kind of time when she folded up like a wood chair against a blank wall in an empty room. She slept for days and days, she felt. She ate a little food. She ate a tablespoon of oatmeal, half a fried egg. She had chili, which she loved. She would eat a bowl of that whenever they gave it to her.

Somebody really strong sat there in Patty Ann's place. Somebody came around lunchtime and afternoon, until Maylene got home.

"She should be in school," somebody said.

"You needn't stay with her. Andrew will stay," her mama said.

"That's not what I mean. I mean, she would get better quicker if she had other things to think about."

"Not as long as my sister keeps up the business."

"Andrew says they've locked her out."

"Yes," Maylene said. "I wonder what she will do next? It's been six weeks."

Cammy woke up and the man was rocking her in the rocking chair. Her legs were so long, they nearly dangled to the floor.

"I'm not a baby," she told him.

He smiled. But she got up anyway. Stood there, with her back to him, looking out the window. Somebody was peeking in through the window. Then, somebody started hollering and banging away on the door.

"Aunt Effie," Cammy said, finally. "Mama? Mama?"

"What is it?" Her mama came in the living room.

"It's your sister," the man said.

"Are you my daddy?"

"Yes."

"Do you want me to go stop her?" he said to Maylene.

"Better you than me," Cammy's mama said. "No telling what I might do to her if I lose my temper."

Cammy heard what Aunt Effie was saying. She just didn't listen to it. She let it go inside her with Patty Ann.

"Nobody is going to forget!" Aunt Effie shouted. "Nobody is going to forget! You think just because L-O-D is gone--my baby isn't gone. She's inside this house. You won't forget what you done. None of you will forget."

Her dad went to the door.

"I want you off this property right now," the man, her dad, said. "You leave the child alone. She didn't do anything."

And then Effie Lee lashed out at all the things Cammy had done to Patty Ann, especially the day of the rain, when Cammy had run from Aunt Effie's house.

"I don't want to hear it. She's a child," her dad said. "They are all children. Your mistake is to mix in with their childishness. We all sympathize with you and your terrible loss. Believe me. But you are a grown woman. Act like it."

Effie Lee hollered, "But they want to forget. They leave me nothing!"

"If you don't go right now, I will call an ambulance to take you to the hospital," said the man who was Cammy's dad.

Instead, Maylene called Andrew, who brought

Richie. Richie had been cold sober since his little sister died.

"Mom?" he said. "Mom, come, let me take you home." That seemed to quiet her somewhat. But she kept on crying. Cammy could tell that she was going away from the house, down the sidewalk.

"Why's my dad here?" Cammy wanted to know.

"To help us out," Maylene said. "I can't take off so much time. He likes coming to see you."

The man came back into the house. The only noise now was inside Cammy's head. He sat down in the chair. She was standing next to the big old rocker, rocking it with her hand. She wondered if Patty Ann was sitting in the rocking chair. She didn't think so; she couldn't see her there. But you never know, Cammy thought.

"Do you feel all right?" the man asked.

"You're my dad," Cammy answered. She thought, I feel all wrong. But there were things she wouldn't say.

"I'm afraid we haven't had a chance to know one another very much. My fault," he said, and smiled.

Big, sandy man, Cammy thought. Sandy hair, sandy skin. Sandy shirt and khaki pants. Light brown buckskin shoes. "Why'd you all quit?" she asked him, curious. She glanced toward the door her mama had gone through. She could smell food cooking.

"What? Oh. You mean your mom and me. Why, I blamed her, I guess, and she blamed me. Either way, we couldn't get along."

"I'm the blame," Cammy whispered. A moment passed and tears rolled down her face. She went over to the man and leaned her head on his shoulder.

"I made you cry. Cammy, I'm sorry."

No. She tried to stop the tears. And her face turned red. Shaking her head. Everything was so wrong and sad.

The man understood. He nodded, saying, "I know. We often hurt the ones we love."

"But I didn't mean to hurt her. Oh, it's my fault. But I didn't mean it!"

"No. No, Cammy. You didn't do anything. It was an accident."

"No it wasn't. She wanted me to be sorry. And I am!"

Cammy cried and cried.

He held her, smoothed her hair. "You are my daughter. I'm your dad and I say you're not to blame. No child drowns to hurt somebody."

Finally, Cammy said, "I think Patty Ann did, to make us hurt for her."

"Oh, Cammy, I don't think so. I think it was an accident."

"You didn't see her face," she said. Then Cammy covered her eyes. She couldn't stand up any longer.

"Maylene?" he called. Her mama came and picked her up. Struggled with her up the stairs.

"I'll take her," he said. But Maylene said no. Wouldn't let Cammy go. Cammy clung to her for dear life. She hated going upstairs to be all alone in her room. Such awful things happened in her room now.

Cammy felt as if she lived only snatches of her days. Pictures and snap shots. She remembered some things. At last, she felt well enough to go back to school. But before she did, two things happened.

8 🌿 They went on a long car ride. She and her mama, Andrew and the man who was her dad. Her dad drove the car. Andrew sat up front beside him. Her mama and she sat in the backseat. The car belonged to her dad. It was the prettiest place inside that car. The seat felt like a cloud under her. Cammy ran her hand along the deep plush of it.

She didn't ask where they were going. Andrew told her, turning around in his seat. "We're going to see your cousin."

Cammy ducked her head and closed her eyes.

"Andrew, for heaven's sake," her mama said. "We're going to see L-O-D today, honey. Isn't that nice?"

Cammy didn't say much. She was glad Elodie was the cousin she was going to see. Migrant child laborer. She'd heard that somewhere. It didn't tell what Elodie was, really. Elodie was really somebody with part of somebody else inside her. The way Cammy had part of the same somebody else inside her.

When they got there, they stopped in front of a little house. It didn't look too migrant to Cammy. It was in a little town. Seemed that Elodie's mom could live there until the spring. Cammy saw Elodie after such a long time, and the back of her mind woke up. She felt more herself than she had in weeks.

The house was stuffy, although the day was cool outside in the fall air. So they sat on a wood bench on this back stoop. There was a narrow piece of yard with no grass, just caked, hard ground. There was a clothesline with nothing on it. It was early Sunday morning, when they got there, just time to go to church. So all was quiet around the many little houses like Elodie's.

"You look nice," Elodie said to Cammy.

"So do you, too," Cammy said back. Elodie had on new Goodwill clothes. They were both dressed for Sunday, although they wouldn't go to church.

"How's school?" asked Elodie.

"Okay, I guess. I haven't gone much," Cammy said.

"I'm so behind because of the work," Elodie said, "I might as well quit."

"Try to stick it out," Cammy said. And wondered at herself for saying that.

"Maybe," Elodie said.

"You look a lot better," Cammy said.

"I get about as much potatoes and beans as I want," Elodie said, seriously. "We picked a lot of apples. I love my mom's applesauce. At the Christian Shelter we ate cow's tongue. It made me vomit."

"This fall? You pick a lot of apples now?" Cammy asked, interested.

"Yes."

"Do you mind, picking things?" Cammy said.

"I don't mind it," Elodie said, after a pause. "I get to be with my mom and her friends. There's some few other kids. But they are tough busters, so I stay away from them. There's a recreation place that they let us go to if we behave. I take off my shoes and go barefoot on the slick floors there. I behave, me and another kid, so we get to go. I stay away from water, though. Streams and things like that."

"That's good."

"But kids still make fun of me because I'm a picker. They laugh at me and my mom," Elodie explained.

"They should be ashamed," Cammy said. She found out that she felt for Elodie, that she liked her a lot. She liked looking into her face. That was the way you looked at Elodie. You had to peer into her, it seemed like. Slide deep into her eyes that were shiny and black. Cammy didn't think she'd ever

looked that closely at Elodie before now. Elodie
had been the one peering at her. It was nice to have
a cousin again you could look straight at, Cammy
decided.

Before they left, after eating lunch and talking to
Elodie's mom in the small kitchen, Elodie said just
to Cammy, "I'm okay."

"Me, too," said Cammy, although she knew it
wasn't the truth. Shyly they smiled at one another.
"Hope you can come home next summer," Cammy
added.

Elodie's chin quivered so much, she couldn't
speak.

"It wasn't your fault," Cammy said, finally. "She
wanted to save you, so she did."

Elodie nodded. "But I thought she'd save herself,
too," she said.

They locked arms, walking a ways around the little house. They were like true friends. "I'll come to
see you again sometime, if I can," Cammy said.

"Okay," Elodie said.

"I saw her go down," Cammy said at the last. "I
told everybody I didn't but I did. It was just—I
couldn't believe it was happening. She looked right
at me."

"She looked at all us," Elodie said.

"Are you sure?" Cammy asked.

"She was just looking at us all. I looked back and
saw her. She knew all us was too far away to help
her," Elodie said. "Then, she forgave us."

"Are you sure?" Cammy said again.

Elodie nodded. "Mama said so. Mama says she's with Jesus now."

A little while later, Cammy and her family went home. Before they left, Cammy saw the way Elodie looked up at Cammy's dad. Cammy took hold of his hand just to prove who he was to her. He squeezed her hand, bent down and kissed the top of her head in front of everybody. Cammy kept her eyes on her shoes. But, boy, it made her proud to have this man so tall who was also her dad. Sandy man.

Cammy forgot most of it before they were half-way home. She would recall it though, in days to come. But for now, things flitted in and out of her mind. Night and her room were always in the back of her head.

She recalled on the long ride home that neither she nor Elodie had mentioned Patricia Ann by name. But no matter who brought up the subject, they both knew at once who they were talking about.

Snatches of memories, snapshots. Cammy could keep nothing in mind for long. She had a big empty hole inside, she told Andrew one time. She had been lying on the couch. She often lay there now, rather than going up into her room. She avoided her room as much as possible. Once in a while, she woke up with Patty Ann sitting on the cot, but not so often.

"Andrew, take that cot away," she told her

brother one time. He took it away that very night. And that night, she slept the night through until just before the first light of dawn. She awoke and thought she saw Patty Ann leave the room. *"Bye, enemy."*

"You don't scare me, kid," was what was in Cammy's mind to tell her dead cousin. But she never said it. Still, she had the presence in the dreaming to think that. Almost bold, like her old self. It made her feel better, dreaming, too.

One time, Cammy was lying on the couch just under wakefulness and still sleepy. The TV was on to daytime soaps. Snatches, when she'd been sick to her stomach. Somebody called a doctor because her mama wondered about her appendix. He came and said, no, nothing like that. Just grief, whatever that meant.

Good grief, was what Cammy thought.

"I don't think she's ever coming out of it," Andrew had said.

She had wanted to say, "Oh, shut up," but had felt too sick to say anything.

After a long kind of time, the second thing happened.

She heard a sound she couldn't identify. Heard her brother and her dad grunting, lifting something. Then, she heard something smoothly turning, it seemed like. She sat up before she was quite awake. She thought she was up in her room. She thought Patty Ann was there. But when she opened her eyes, everybody was smiling. "See?" said her mama, Maylene. They were all in the living room. Cammy was sitting on the couch.

"See, I bet you never thought of it," Andrew told her.

Her dad grinned from ear to ear.

"A big surprise just for you!" said Maylene. "And home for supper. We'll have a fine time, too."

Cammy sat there. She stared and stared. She couldn't recognize, she couldn't tell. All so many snatches of memory rose up like little twigs on a whirlpool. It was as if a whole lifetime had gone by and she'd forgot what it was all about until somehow, it had come back. It was shocking, the way it would be if Patty Ann came back up out of the bluety.

And now she recalled. Couldn't believe she'd so completely forgotten, but she had.

"Fooled ya!" Gram Tut piped from the wheelchair. They had rolled her in and she'd kept her eyes squinted shut on the shade within. She shot them open just before she spoke these words to Cammy. It had been a hard trip for her. But she'd made it to come bring back her Cammy. They'd told her all about it.

"Poor baby," Gram Tut had said. They'd not thought to bring her, but had thought to take Cammy to her. "No," she'd said. "That baby has to see me come all the way over there." And so she had. It had been a hard struggle, their getting her

cleaned up and dressed. Getting her into a wheelchair comfortably. Getting the chair and her into
the Care van with Maylene riding with her to reas-
sure her. And getting her out and into Maylene's,
her daughter's house.

Lordy.

Cammy slid from the couch and came over next
to her blessed Gram. "Oh. Oh," she murmured
from somewhere deep in her heart. She came as
close as she could, leaning on hard metal to plant a
gentle, sweet kiss on Gram Tut's sagging cheek.
Cammy's chest was just full of love and her eyes
filled with it, too. "You came all this way?" she
whispered. "Just to see me!"

Tut's arms went shakily around Cammy to em-
brace her. Her breath sounded like a dry rasping.
And her fingers felt just like withered, dry leaves.
Cammy didn't mind Gram's scratchy skin. She always did like winter and fallen leaves in the snow.

"Lordy," Tut gasped, "I'm wore out. Child, take
me to the kitchen. Let's get this meal done!"

"Well, Mom, we got time, you can rest some.
You want to lie down?" Maylene asked her own
mama.

"Just sit a minute, is all." Tut paused, breathing.
"Me and my baby girl." She took Cammy's hand,
patted it. When she touched the child, it was like a
blaze of summer coming into her hands. Like her
curtains, breeze making them swell up with day and
heat.

"Oh," Tut said. "I coulda died. All that time, you

forgot me, didn't you?" she said to Cammy. They went into the kitchen.

There was never any nonsense between them. Cammy told the truth.

"It was all so awful, Gram."

"Tell it," Gram said, wheezing.

"Don't you die on me, too," Cammy whined.

"Cammy, stop it," her mama, Maylene said.

Andrew came in with armloads of groceries. Set them on the counter. Maylene began putting the bags' contents into the cupboards. Cammy's dad came in, spoke kindly to Gram Tut.

"You know him?" Cammy asked.

"Knew him before I knew you," Gram said.

Cammy thought about that a long time. She sat in the chair closest to Gram's wheelchair. She had her hands folded in her lap and her knees tight together. She never took her eyes from Gram's face. They drank in each other.

Gram rested and had something to drink before she got to talking just to Cammy. Although everyone was walking around or sitting now and again at the table with them, nobody bothered them or cut in on what they were talking about.

Gram touched Cammy's hair. "Pretty stuff," she said. Cammy set still and let her Gram make over her. "She got her daddy's mouth, you know," Tut decided, at one point. "Gimmie some more of that apple," she said to Andrew. She was too tired, and her hands trembled with age.

Andrew fixed Gram Tut apple juice with a straw.

Cammy held the glass for her so she could keep on resting herself. Gram sucked it up through the straw.

"They didn't think I could get here . . . but I did," she told Cammy. Swallowing, breathing quickly.

"You're not too tired?" Cammy asked.

"Lord no! One day . . . I'll sleep forever. So will you!"

Cammy thought about that. She thought about Patty Ann and forever. She sighed. "My cousin died," she told Gram Tut, as if she didn't know.

"Well, yes," Tut said. "Terrible thing. Just awful." A pause while she rested, and then: "One day, you look around . . . everybody you know is dead. Happened to me. Happens, if you live . . . too long!"

She smiled at Cammy. But Cammy was listening hard and hadn't time to smile. Maylene stood off a ways. Cammy knew she was there. Maylene never interrupted. Even though Gram Tut could shock her by what she said.

"Effie's baby dies," Tut said. "Too soon, too soon. Now *me*, it'd be too late!" she laughed.

But now she looked hard at Cammy. "You got to stop this," she said. "We, left behind . . . have to go ahead on." She stopped to breathe, easier, it seemed to Cammy. Someone to talk to always helped Tut to find her words.

Cammy leaned close to Gram and put her hands over Gram's on the chair rests. "I saw her go down.

The bluety just took her out of sight. Where is she, Gram?" She'd been worried about that.

"Well," Gram Tut said, and paused. "Her body's caught down there somewheres . . . I suspect," Gram said. "Never to come up again."

Maylene sucked in her breath. Cammy heard her dad's voice. "Don't," he said to Maylene. "Stay out of it. She's fine," he said.

"She won't come back," Cammy said.

"No, baby," Gram said. "Nothing for you to worry over. You've been dreaming, is all. Scared yourself. Don't take on so anymore. She's gone.

"We live. We die." Tut smiled, looked off, dreamily. Just when Cammy thought she'd truly gone off, her Gram said, "Pray it won't be hard. Sometimes it is. Sometimes not." Tut spoke slowly but clearly. "It's not our place . . . to question His mystery."

Cammy was pressed against her Gram. Her eyes closed. Her ear and face hard on Tut's thin chest. She could hear the old heart of her. It beat slow, steady; every now and then, it gave a slight roll before it beat right on.

She's gonna go, too, Cammy thought, and could have cried. But she wouldn't. "What's to eat?" she said, huskily.

"Now there's an appetite . . . through thick and thin," said Gram Tut.

"I'm here, Mom, whenever you want to start cooking," said Maylene.

"Start now?" asked Gram.

"Nooo," Cammy moaned and held on tightly to her old love, so fragile.

"In a minute, then," Gram said, and put her chin on Cammy's head with untold gentleness.

It was a good, long day among them, in that house of Maylene's. Maylene cooked. Andrew and Cammy's dad did whatever Maylene wanted. Often, Cammy caught her dad looking concerned at her. That made her happy, she wasn't so sure why.

"I been seeing you a lot lately," she said to him after a while.

"Getting to be a habit," Maylene murmured.

The man, her dad, stared at Cammy's mama. He thrust his hands into his pockets and looked down at the floor. Maylene smiled to herself.

Cammy saw it all and felt them winding tightly together among shade trees.

"Winter's coming," she warned her Gram.

"I know it, too," Tut said. "Listen, take what comes. Put a focus on . . . each little thing comes before you. Just one thing at a time. That's how it's done. Always be ready. I'm ready."

Tut would have her dinner made in the oven. So that was how she directed Maylene to do it. Maylene did it exactly as Gram Tut commanded. Cammy watched closely. She focused herself, just as Gram said she should, on each little thing. When Tut spoke, Cammy watched her lips and felt her words fill up her insides. When Maylene moved, Cammy was right there on her elbow. She peered into the oven, into the oblong glass oven dish Maylene had filled with chicken parts. There was yellow and green pepper. There was red tomatoes cut up. There was salt and pepper and spices like oregano and garlic sprinkled on the chicken. There was water and cooking wine mixed together, just enough to cover the bottom well, about a half inch. There was paprika to help in the browning, Gram Tut said. Later, she would have Maylene add ketsup, vinegar and honey.

Cammy saw how the chicken was prepared. She thought of nothing else. When the oven door closed on the food, cooking it, she turned her attention to the next thing.

"Now, turn up to 350 degrees," Gram said. "Maylene, hurry some. I got to lie down awhile."

While the chicken cooked, and Gram Tut napped, Cammy and Andrew made salad. The onion scent went up Cammy's nose and made tears in her eyes. Andrew wet a towel for her and she washed her eye rims with it. Her dad went away and came back with sheet cake and ice cream just before the food was ready.

Gram came in, in her wheelchair, looking refreshed. They sat down to the finest meal Cammy had in a long time.

"Just like it's been fried," her dad said.

"Well, I had Maylene add some brown sugar. Forgot it until the last minute," Tut said.

"And the ketsup, vinegar and honey," Maylene said, "I remembered them, Mom."

"Well, I'm thankful for that. It tastes fine," Gram

said. But used to puréed food, she ate very little. She ate some gravy and thin slivers of chicken. Ice cream. Cammy mixed some with the cake and Gram ate that.

"Gram, you seem like you grew younger while you slept." Cammy told her.

Her dad smiled on her.

"Expect I did," Gram said. "Sleep's known to work wonders. So is home."

The kitchen seemed small and full, Cammy thought. It was warm, with all of them crushed tightly around the kitchen table. Cammy was squeezed between her Dad and Gram Tut's chair. She didn't mind. She focused on eating and tasted every single bit of it as though she never tasted anything before. She drank tons of ice tea. And when that was gone, she drank two full glasses of ice water.

"Lordy," Gram Tut said. "Child is growing before my eyes."

It was a long, full time over supper. Cammy had two slices of cake and two helpings of two kinds of ice cream. "Not even my birthday, either," she said, her mouth full.

"I love sweet stuff," said Tut.

"I do, too," said Cammy.

"This whole house has got a sweet tooth," Andrew said.

Everything came to a close about eight o'clock. Cammy went with them to put Gram back in the

Care. Maylene called for the Care van. Cammy and Andrew and Maylene rode in it with Gram and the driver. When they got there, Cammy saw that her dad had driven up behind to take them back. But first, they saw Gram in. Care givers placed Gram and her chair on a chair lift out of the van. They rolled her inside and down the hall, past the nurses' station. It was the first time in a long time that Cammy had not sneaked into the place.

Televisions were on in all the rooms. Folks were strolling down the halls in their chairs, those who could get around. Old Otha came into view, and peered at them.

"You finish your hog hut?" Cammy hollered at him, loud, so he could hear.

"Oh, kid, hush up!" he said, out of sorts from the day's ending. But he recognized her voice all the same.

Cammy laughed. Old people always said they were going to do things but forgot to do them.

They stood in the hall while an aide got Gram ready for bed. It took about fifteen minutes. Her dad came in and stood beside her at the railing. Cammy took his hand and placed it against her cheek. Suddenly, she just couldn't get enough of him.

"Can I come to where you and Andrew work?"

"Want to see my office?" the man said.

"Can I?"

"I'll take you and Andrew out to lunch."

"When!"

"Tomorrow, if you go to school. I'll come and get you."

"Swell!" she said.

Cammy had a thought hit her all of a sudden. I'll put my focus on him. There won't be anybody sad anymore. My hocus focus!

He squeezed her shoulder, made warm shivers around her neck.

He'll be just like Andrew and Mama. Gram Tut and all I love.

The door to Tut's room opened. The aide came out, smiled at them as he went by. They went in. Gram was propped up in bed. Cammy climbed the rail, planted a kiss on her good Gram's cheek. Gram puckered her mouth like she might cry, so Cammy kissed it. Made Tut smile.

"Listen!" Tut murmured.

"So, what?" Cammy said in her ear.

But Gram was so tired, she fell asleep before she could think to say something. Cammy didn't mind. She never even thought, are you a dead doornail?

She was thinking, when Gram goes, I'll like to die, too. Just the same as with Patty Ann. With a big hole in me. Even more. Just all empty.

I don't know how it ever happened, any of it. Cammy sighed. People dying is awful, awful sad. They never ever will come back, too. Patty Ann. Just nightmares.

But he's mine who I never knew. My dad. He's so nice to me.

Things. Go down deep. Patty Ann. And all the feelings I liked to buried. But sometimes, they come up again. They come clean.

All at once she watched Gram's chest move slowly up and down.

That's the focus. In, out, she thought. One time, it'll have to stop. And waking and sleeping. One time, you don't ever even wake up again.

Cammy swallowed hard. Took a deep breath.

Well, keep your eyes open. Look while you can. Gram! I love you much. That's it, then.

I get it, now.